It Felt Strange
to Deliberately Re-enter Hell . . .

They say you can't go home again. But you can return to hell if you're crazy and you deliberately take a one-way ticket to Phobos.

We didn't encounter opposition for the first fifteen minutes. We did encounter a functional lift that appeared to have been repaired with pieces of a steam demon. I didn't like the idea of using it, but Hidalgo made the decision.

The makings of a reception committee waited for us at the bottom. Occupying the center of the room was an almost intact spider-mind. All that was missing was the head. In the smashed dome on top, where normally resided the evil brain-face, two spinies were eating.

One of the imps looked up from his meal. Bits of gore dripped off the white horns sticking out from its body.

Fly raised his BFG 9000 at the same instant the imp threw one of his patented fireballs . . .

DOOM Novels Available from Pocket Books

KNEE-DEEP IN THE DEAD by Dafydd ab Hugh and
  Brad Linaweaver
HELL ON EARTH by Dafydd ab Hugh and Brad Linaweaver
INFERNAL SKY by Dafydd ab Hugh and Brad Linaweaver
ENDGAME by Dafydd ab Hugh and Brad Linaweaver

INFERNAL SKY

A Novel by Dafydd ab Hugh and Brad Linaweaver

Based on *Doom,* from id Software

POCKET BOOKS
New York   London   Toronto   Sydney   Tokyo   Singapore

This book is a work of fiction. Names, characters, places and
incidents are products of the authors' imagination or are used
fictitiously. Any resemblance to actual events or locales or persons,
living or dead, is entirely coincidental.

This work is based upon the computer software games DOOM™
and DOOM II™. DOOM © 1993 id Software, Inc. All rights
reserved. DOOM II © 1994 id Software, Inc. All rights reserved.

An *Original* Publication of POCKET BOOKS

 POCKET BOOKS, a division of Simon & Schuster Inc.
1230 Avenue of the Americas, New York, NY 10020

ISBN: 0-671-52563-8

First Pocket Books printing June 1996

10 9 8 7 6 5 4 3 2 1

DOOM™ and DOOM II™ are trademarks of id Software, Inc.

POCKET and colophon are registered trademarks of
Simon & Schuster Inc.

Cover art by Romas Kukalis

Printed in the U.S.A.

To Arnold Schwarzenegger
(with no ulterior motives)

INFERNAL SKY

Prologue

"Why are there monsters?"

An exhausted woman looked at her little boy, who had asked the question that was burning in her own mind. His voice didn't tremble. She reached over to wipe his face. They were not wearing camo right now, and the smudges of dirt were only dirt. It wasn't right for a ten-year-old to be a seasoned veteran of war, she thought, but all of the human survivors on Earth understood what it meant to fight for their lives against alien invaders.

A long time ago, when she was ten, her only question was "Are there real monsters?" What a wonderful world that had been, a sane world where nightmares stayed where they belonged, lodged in the gray matter between the ears. Only in dreams would you encounter giant floating heads that spit ball lightning; angry crimson minotaurs; shambling human zombies fresh from their own death; flying metal skulls with razor teeth dripping blood; ghosts colder than the grave; fifteen-foot-tall demons with heavy artillery in place of hands; obscenely fat shapes, only vaguely humanoid, that could crush the life from the strongest man in a matter of seconds; and, finally, there was the special horror of the mechanical spider bodies with things inside them that were far worse than any arachnid.

There was no way to answer David, no explanation for why dream shapes crawled across the land that once was a country called the United States on a planet called Earth.

She thanked God that her son was still alive. After her husband died, there were only three of them. Three. The number made her cry. They weren't three for long.

She'd never had time to grieve over the man she loved. The monsters didn't give her any time at all. Her daughter, Lisa, had been thirteen.

At least her husband had died bravely, ripped apart by the steel legs of a spider-thing. For a brief moment the woman had caught a glimpse of the evil face peering out from the dome mounted on top of the mechanical body. She couldn't stop herself crying out! Her husband couldn't hear her. But the spider-thing heard everything.

She still blamed herself for that momentary loss of control. Her daughter might have been alive today if Mom hadn't freaked out and drawn the attention of the mechanical horror at that instant. The sounds of the monster were the worst part as it headed toward the remaining members of the family. The heavy pounding would stay in the woman's head forever, along with the screaming of her terrified daughter— right before the girl's head was torn off.

A human head makes a sound like nothing else when it's played with and crushed.

She thanked God David hadn't seen what happened to his sister. But lately she found herself wondering if she should ever give thanks for anything again. Although she'd always been religious, she was forgetting how to pray. She told herself it was like the Book of Job: everyone was being tested as everything was taken away. But the Book of Job didn't have spider-things in it.

"I don't know why there are monsters," she said, finally responding to her son's question. "These creatures come from outer space. We've learned some important things about them."

"What?" he asked.

She looked out the window of the basement where they'd been hiding for the past week. It was a clear night, and she could see the stars. She used to feel peaceful when she looked at the night sky; now she hated those eternal spots of fire.

"We've learned they can die," she said quietly. "They are not what they appear to be. They're not real demons."

"Demons? Like the minister used to tell us about?"

She smiled and ran her fingers through what was left of her son's hair. "They can't take you to hell," she said. "They can't do anything to your soul. Real demons don't need guns or rockets. And, as I said, real demons don't die."

David looked out the window for a while and then said, "But they *are* monsters."

"Yes," she agreed. "We have to believe in them now. But I want you to promise me something."

"What, Mom?"

She pulled him close and tried not to notice his missing arm. "There's something more important than believing in monsters, David. Our minister

3

thought we were in End Times. He didn't even try to fight the spider-things, except with his cross and his Bible. But they can be fought with weapons. The human race will prevail! If we have faith in ourselves. I want you to promise that you'll always believe in heroes."

"Heroes will save us," he echoed her. The two of them stood together for a long time, looking out the window at the blind white stars.

1

"So how did you guys escape from that death trap?" asked Master Gunnery Sergeant Mulligan.

"With *one mighty leap,* sir . . ." I began, but he didn't like my tone of voice.

"Oh, don't give me that, Corporal Taggart," he said. "You guys are holding out on me. You can't tell me you were trapped near the top of a forty-story building in downtown L.A. with all those freakin' demons after you, and then just leave it there."

When he said "you guys," he meant we didn't have to call him sir. Not here, not now. "That's exactly it," I said with a big grin. "We *left!*"

"We probably ought to tell him," said Arlene sleepily. She stretched like a cat in her beach chair, her breasts seeming to point at the horizon. She'd left her bikini top back at the hotel. The view was spectacular from every angle.

For the last few days we'd been pretending that life had returned to normal. Hawaii was still a stronghold of humanity. On a good day the sky was normal. Blue, blue everywhere, and not a single streak of bilious alien green. The wonderful sun was exactly what it ought to be—yellow, round, and not covered with a new rash of sunspots. At least not today. We'd slapped on plenty of suntan lotion, and we were soaking up the rays.

We weren't going to waste a good day like this. The radar worked. The sonar worked. The brand-new *really good* detection equipment worked, too. Every detection device known to man was in use for sea and sky. We almost felt safe. So the three of us decided to play. The master gun was a great guy. Off duty, he liked to be called George. He didn't mind being teased, either.

Hawaii Base employed the services of a number of scientists and doctors. I'll never forget Arlene's reaction when they said that Albert was going to be all right, despite his having taken a face full of acidic imp puke. Best of all, he wasn't going to be blind. Once Arlene heard that, she allowed herself to genuinely relax. I was damned glad that our Mormon buddy had pulled through. He'd proved to be one hell of a marine all the way from Salt Lake City to the monster rally in L.A. What was more, he'd proved to be a true friend.

The docs said they could bring Ken back all the way. Not that Ken had been exactly dead; but he might as well have been when the alternative was to exist as a cybermummy, serving the alien warlords who had turned Earth into a charnel house. He'd already helped us against the enemy by communicating to us through the computer setup our teenage whiz kid, Jill, had thrown together in record time. Arlene and I had used every kind of heavy artillery against the demonic invaders, first on Phobos, then on Deimos, and finally on good old terra firma. Jill had taught us that a good hacker was invaluable in a war against monsters.

That's why we were so happy when we landed at Oahu and found not only a fully operational military establishment but also a prime collection of scientists. Arlene and I were warriors. Our task was to buy the human race that most precious of all commodities: time. Victory would require a lot more than muscle and guts; it would require all the brainpower left on the old mud ball. We needed to learn everything about these creatures that had brought doom to the human race. And then we would pay them back . . . big time.

Yeah, Arlene and I felt good about the men and women in white coats. For one thing, they said it was okay to swim. It had been such a long time since I'd plunged my body into something as reasonable as cool salt water that I hardly cared about their reports. If it didn't look like a pool of green or red sludge, that was all I needed to know. The Pacific Ocean looked fine to yours truly, especially today as we enjoyed fresh salt breezes that would never carry a whiff of sour-lemon zombie stench.

Jill had decided to spend the day working instead of joining us. One of the best research scientists had taken her under his wing. Albert had gone to town. Of course, the "town" was every bit as much a high-security military zone as the "hotel." (I'd never had better barracks.) After what we'd all been through, this place was heaven on earth. The other islands were also secure, but they were not set up for the easy life we enjoyed here.

As I took a sip of my Jack Daniel's, I reflected on the miracle that I felt secure enough to risk taking a drink. For the past month of nonstop hell, first in space and then on Earth, I wouldn't have risked dulling my senses for a second, or saturating my bodily tissues with anything but stimulants. Earth could still count on Corporal Flynn Taggart, Fox Company, Fifteenth Light Drop Infantry Regiment, United States Marine Corps, 888-23-9912. I was in for the duration.

Glancing over at Arlene, I was pleased to see that she was healing nicely. Even though we treated each other as best buddies instead of potential lovers, I wasn't blind. Even the flaming balls of demon mucus hadn't burned out my capacity to see that PFC Arlene Sanders had the perfect female body, at least by my standards: slender but with well-cut muscles and with everything in ideal proportion.

Sometimes Arlene did her mind-reading act. Now she glanced in my direction and gave me the once-over. I guess similar thoughts were going through her mind. More than our bodies were healing. Our souls had taken a beating. When we first arrived on the island, and Arlene could finally accept that we had found a pocket of safety, she had tried to sleep; but she was so stressed out that only drugs could take her under. Even then she'd wake up every half hour, just as exhausted as before.

I wasn't doing too well when we first arrived, either. But I was too worried about her to pay attention to my own aches and pains. She said she'd never felt so empty. She couldn't stop worrying about Albert. So I told her all the things she'd said to me when I was down. About how it was our turn to man the barricades and we had to keep going, past every obstacle of terror and fatigue and despair. Then I shook her hard and told her to come out of it because we were on vacation in Hawaii, dammit!

Master Gun Mulligan was an invaluable help throughout this period of adjustment. He was an old friend none of us had ever met before. You meet that kind in the service when you're lucky. It makes up for all the Lieutenant Weems types.

Of course, you should only tease a friend so far. The master gun had every right to know how we'd pulled off our "impossible" escape from the old Disney Tower. He just had the bad luck to be caught between Arlene Sanders and Fly Taggart in a game of who-gives-in-first.

"All right," said Mulligan, half to himself, slipping a little as he climbed out of his beach chair. He was a big man, and he was right at the weight limit. He didn't really have to worry about it, though. No one would worry about the minutiae of military rules for a good long time. If you could fight and follow orders, the survivors of civilization as we know it would sure as hell find you a task in this human's army.

Mulligan planted his feet firmly, put his hands on his sizable hips, and gave us his personal ultimatum. "Here's the deal," he said. "I'm going back to the 'hotel' to bring us a six-pack of ice-cold beer. When I return, I have every intention of sharing the wealth. That's what will happen if you make me happy. But if you want to see a really unhappy marine, then don't tell me how the two of you escaped from a forty-story building with a mob of devils after your blood when the two of you are in a sealed room, the only exit to which is one window offering you a sheer drop to certain doom."

"You've expressed yourself with admirable clarity,"

said Arlene. She loved showing off that college education. Didn't matter to me if she ever graduated. She'd picked up plenty of annoying traits for me to forgive.

"Yeah, right!" he said.

"We'll take your suggestion under advisement." Arlene laid it on thicker.

"Bullshit!" said Mulligan, turning his back on us and storming off down the beach.

"One, two, three, four," I said.

"We love the Marine Corps," he boomed back at us, still headed toward his—and maybe our—beer.

"I think we'd better tell him," I said.

"He wants to know who the big hero is," she replied. "So he can get an autograph." I noted that she didn't say "his" or "her."

"You're on," I replied. God, it was fine to sit in the sun, soaking up rays and alcohol, watching the gentle waves rolling in to the shore, seeing an actual seagull once in a while . . . and giving a hard time to a really nice man who was a newfound friend.

Our moment of pure relaxation was interrupted, but not by anything satanic. It was an honor when the highest-ranking officer in Hawaii—and maybe in the human race, for all we knew—strolled over to talk to us while he was off duty. He wasn't our commanding officer, so that made us slightly more at ease when he insisted on it. The way Arlene blushed suggested she would have worn the top to her bikini if she'd expected a visit from the CO of New Pearl Harbor Naval Base, Vice Admiral Kimmel.

"What are you two up to?" asked Admiral Kimmel. We hadn't noticed him walking down the beach. He'd come from the direction where the sun was in our eyes.

"Sir!" came out of our mouths simultaneously and we started to get up.

"As you were, marines." Then he smiled and repeated his pleasantry as if he expected an answer.

"We were unprepared for your surprise attack," Arlene said to the commanding officer and got away with it. He laughed.

The admiral continued standing. Sometimes rank avoids its privileges. He took off his white straw hat and used it to fan himself in the sweltering heat. His thin legs were untouched by the least hint of tan, but there was plenty of color, courtesy of his Bermuda shorts and the tackiest Hawaiian shirt of all time. When he was off duty, he wore this uniform to announce his leisure.

"I'm glad someone of your generation knows the history of her country," the admiral said, complimenting Arlene. "It's a strange coincidence that I have the same name as the admiral who was here when the Japanese bombed Pearl Harbor. How much of our history will be destroyed in this Demon War, even if the human race survives? Guard what is in your head. The history books of the future may be written by you."

Arlene sighed. "When we go back into action I don't think we'll be doing much writing, except for reports."

"Signing off with famous last words," I threw in helpfully. It suddenly occurred to me that I might know something about the admiral that would be news to Arlene, who was the acknowledged expert on science-fiction movies and novels. It would be nice to stump her right here and now on something important.

Before I could get a word out, though, Arlene smiled and said, "Fly, are you familiar with Admiral Kimmel's book? He's a Pearl Harbor revisionist."

Damn! She had done it to me again, making exactly the point I was about to make. With this final proof of Arlene's telepathic ability, I decided in all future combat situations to let her go over the hill first. Especially if there happened to be a steam demon on the other side.

Admiral Kimmel chuckled. "If I hadn't been friends with the late president of the United States, I would never have written that book," he told us, remembering pre-invasion days. The president had died when Washington was captured by the bad guys.

"He was the one who changed my mind about Pearl Harbor," the admiral continued, "not my Japanese wife, as many believe. I believe the evidence proves that top officials in Washington withheld important information from the commanding officers at Pearl Harbor before the Japanese attack in December of 1941. Well, we don't have to worry about that sort of nonsense in this war."

I nodded, adding, "There's no Washington."

As we talked, I noticed that Arlene became more relaxed. We discussed our military backgrounds in the days before the monsters came. I was glad we had a man in charge of the island who had been a division officer on a battleship, and a captain seeing action in the Gulf before that. He'd been doing a shore tour as a commander when the world capsized.

"There's a pleasant sight," he said, pointing at the sea. There was a cloud on the horizon. A small white cloud.

He started to leave and then turned back, his face suddenly as stern as a bust of Julius Caesar. His mouth was his strongest feature as he said, "They won't beat us. It's as if these islands have been given a second chance. There will never be a surprise attack here, not ever again. Let them come, in their thousands or their millions. We're going to teach them that we are worse monsters than they are. This is our world, and we're not giving it up. And it won't stop there. We'll take the battle to them, somewhere, somehow. . . ."

He wanted to keep talking, but he'd run out of words, so his mouth kept working in silence, like a weapon being fired on an empty chamber after the ammo is used up. We both felt the emotion from this strong old man.

Arlene stood up and put her hand on his arm. She helped him regain his composure. The gesture wasn't regulation, but who cared?

For years I'd been asked why a rabid individualist like me had chosen a military life. Some of the people who asked that question understood that I wanted a life with honor, especially after having lived with a father who didn't have a clue. They could even understand someone putting his life on the line for his fellow man. It was individualism that confused them.

I became a marine because I believe in freedom: the old American dream that had defied the nightmares of so many other countries. Every Independence Day I made a point of reading the Declaration of Independence out loud.

I loved my country enough to fight for it. Now we faced an enemy that threatened everything and everyone on the planet. Any military system that had its head stuck up its own bureaucratic ass was finished. Now was the time to adapt or die. Now was the time to really send in the marines!

2

"**I** almost brought you some iced tea," said Mulligan, "with lots of lemon."

Arlene and I both grimaced. "He's getting mean," she said.

"A sadist," I agreed. We'd told the master gun plenty about our adventures, and he had fixated on the way Albert, Jill, Arlene, and I had passed ourselves off as zombies by rubbing rotten lemons and limes all over ourselves. The odor of the zombies had forever spoiled the taste of citrus for me.

" 'Course I could let you have one of these instead," Mulligan continued, holding out two frosty Limbaugh brews, one in each paw.

"The man's getting desperate," I said.

"Who goes first?" asked Arlene, ready to spill the beans; and Mulligan hoped they would be tastier than the typical MRE.

The admiral had left us. He looked like an old beachcomber as he wandered down the beach. I thought about what he'd said—how he'd tied the past and future together with these precious islands as the center of his universe. Maybe they were the center of the universe for all humanity.

"Beers first," I volunteered, holding my hand out.

Mulligan looked as happy as Jill when I let her drive the truck. He passed out the brews and settled his considerable bulk back in his beach chair.

"Once upon a time . . ." I began, but Arlene punched me so hard it made her breasts jiggle very nicely. With that kind of encouragement, I got plenty serious.

"We had to take down the energy wall so Jill could fly out of L.A. and get here," I began. "In the Disney Tower we located a roomful of computers hooked into a collection of alien biotech—"

"Yeah, yeah," Mulligan said impatiently. "I remember all that. Get to the window already!"

So I did.

We were too high. I'd never liked heights, but it seemed best to open the windows.

"We took down the energy wall, at least," I had said over my shoulder. "Jill *must* notice it's gone and start treading air for Hawaii."

Arlene nodded, bleak even in victory. I didn't need alien psionics to know she was thinking of Albert. "The war techies will track her as an unknown rider," added Arlene, "and they'll scramble some jets; they should be able to make contact and talk her down."

"Great. Got a hot plan to talk *us* down?" I asked my buddy.

Arlene shook her head. I had a crazy wish that before Albert was blinded, and before Arlene and I found ourselves in this cul-de-sac, I'd played Dutch uncle to the two lovebirds, complete with blessings and unwanted advice.

Somehow this did not seem the ideal moment to suggest that Arlene seriously study the Mormon faith, or some related religion, if she really loved good old Albert. The sermon went into my favorite mental file, the one marked Later.

She shook her head. "There's no way," she began, "unless . . ."

"Yes?" I asked, trying not to let the sound of slavering monsters outside the door add panic to the atmosphere.

Arlene stared at the door, at the console, then out the window. She went over to the window as if she had all the time in the world and looked straight down. Then up. For some reason, she looked up.

She faced me again, wearing a big, crafty Arlene Sanders smile. "You are not going to believe this, Fly Taggart, but I think—I think I have it. I know how to get us down *and* get us to Hawaii."

I smiled, convinced she'd finally cracked. "Great idea, Arlene. We could use a vacation from all this pressure."

"You don't believe me."

"You're right. I don't believe you."

Arlene smiled slyly. She was using the early-bird-that-got-the-worm-smile. "Flynn Taggart, bring me some duct tape from the toolbox, an armload of computer-switch wiring, and the biggest goddam boot you can find!"

The boot was the hard part.

The screaming, grunting, scraping, mewling, hissing, roaring, gurgling, ripping, and crackling sound effects from beyond the door inspired me to speed up the scavenger hunt. Hurrying back to the window with the items, I saw Arlene leaning out and craning her neck to look up.

"Do you see it?" she asked as I joined her. Clear as

day, there was a window washer's scaffold hanging above us like a gateway to paradise. When the invasion put a stop to mundane activities, all sorts of jobs had been left uncompleted. In this case, it meant quantities of Manila hemp rope dangling like the tentacles of an octopus. A few lengths of chain, with inch-long links, were even more promising than the rope. The chain looked rusted, but I was certain that it would support our weight.

The tentacles started above us and extended well below the fortieth floor—not all the way to the ground, but a lot farther away from the demons in the hallway working so hard to make our acquaintance.

Arlene used the duct tape and the wiring to create a spaghetti ladder that didn't look as if it would hold her weight very long, never mind my extra kilos. But we needed an extra leg up to get over to the ropes.

"Great," I said. "This looks like a job for Fly Taggart."

Before I could clamber out the window, however, her hand was on my arm. "Hold on a minute," she said. "My idea, my mission."

The locked door was rattling like a son of a bitch, and the thought of our entrails decorating the office made me a trifle impatient. That was one kind of spaghetti I could pass over.

"Arlene," I said, as calmly as possible under the circumstances, "I have absolute confidence in you, but this is no time to hose the mission. Let's face it, I have more upper body strength and a greater reach than you do, so I should go first." While I explained the situation, we both worked feverishly to finish our makeshift rope. Then I tied it around my waist.

Naturally I gave her no opportunity to argue. I was

at that window so fast she probably feared for my life. A good way to keep her from staying pissed. I took one mighty leap, making sure she held the other end of the lifeline, and I climbed up and over, where I grabbed hold of the nearest rope and started lowering myself, groaning a bit at the strain and reminding myself that I had all this great upper body strength. I only wished I had more of it to spare.

Once I was on the ropes, I swung myself over to where Arlene could reach them more easily. She clambered out the window over my head and followed my lead.

The annoying voice in the back of my head chose that precise moment to start an argument. Damned voice had a lousy sense of timing.

Getting tired, are you? Feeling a bit middle-aged around the chest area? Old heart hanging in there? The arms are strong from all those push-ups and pull-ups, but how's the grip? Your hands are weaker than they used to be, aren't they? You know, you haven't had these injuries looked at. . . .

"Nothing a blue sphere couldn't fix up," I muttered.

Medikits aren't good enough for you, Corporal? You'd rather trust in that alien crap, huh? And how do you know that you and Arlene weren't altered in some diabolical manner when your lives were saved in that infernal blue light?

"I'm hanging from a freakin' rope and you choose this moment to worry about that?" I shouted.

"Fly, are you all right?" Arlene called down.

"Okay," I called back, feeling like a complete idiot. Normally I don't argue out loud with the voice in my head.

"Don't go weird on me now," she said. "If I fall, I want my strong he-man to catch li'l ol' me."

"No problemo," I promised. "But I think we're getting enough exercise as things stand." Well, at least I'd convinced her I was playing with a full deck again.

As if life had become too easy for us, the door in the office flew off with such force that it smashed through what was left of the window and went sailing in the direction of the freeway. The door was as black and twisted as if someone had turned it into burned toast and tossed it in the trash.

The first monster to peer out the window, if black dots count as eyes, was one of the things Arlene had wisely dubbed a fire eater. It must have only recently joined the other pukes and taken care of the door problem for them. In a flash it could solve the rope problem, too, burning our lifeline to cinders. We didn't have a fire extinguisher this time.

Fire Guy wasn't alone, either. He was the gate-crasher, bringing with him a whole monster convention. They'd be pouring down the ropes after us like molasses on a string if we didn't do something fast.

I stopped the story there because I wanted to finish my beer, and because I had my eye on another can of Limbaugh. The master gun had brought a six-pack, so with the aid of higher arithmetic, I figured I had another one coming.

"And?" asked Mulligan, fire in his eye; and the way his mouth was working you could say fire in the hole, too.

"As the fire eater was getting ready to burn our ropes—and you can always tell an attack is coming by the way its skin bubbles and its body shimmers like a heat mirage in the desert—I swung out and then came in hard, kicking in a window with one try. In the remaining seconds I pulled the rope taut and Arlene shimmied down into my arms as tongues of flame raced after her. But we'd made it to a much lower floor. We had a twelve-story head start, so we booked."

"Story is right!" thundered Mulligan. "I've never heard so much bullshit!"

For one grim moment I wasn't at all sure I'd be getting my second beer.

3

"**H**old on," said Mulligan, guarding his small ocean of beer as the larger ocean sent armies of waves to die on the beach, "I'm not buying it. When I was a kid, I was in the Boy Scouts. I carried the heaviest knapsack on camping trips. I won all the merit badges. I was a good scout, but other kids still beat me up and teased me all the time. Do you want to guess why?"

"Why?" asked Arlene, genuinely interested and not the least bit annoyed by the mysterious direction the conversation was taking.

"Partly because I was a chunky kid, but also

because I loved comic books. They thought I was gullible or something. They thought I'd believe damn near anything. But I'm telling you, Fly"—he turned those cold blue eyes on me—"this story of yours is bullshit."

"You believe the part about his starting to lose his mind while he was on the rope, don't you?" asked Arlene.

"Well . . ." Mulligan began.

"I left nothing out of my gospel rendition," I said.

"Especially not the verisimilitude," Arlene threw in.

"Huh?" came the response from both Mulligan and me.

"Still sounds bogus to me," concluded the master gun, inhaling the rest of his brew.

"That's because it didn't happen that way," said Arlene. "I'll give you the authentic version—for another beer."

"Yeah, right," the sergeant said morosely, but he handed her a beer, and she started her engines.

"With one mighty leap . . ." she began.

George Mulligan groaned.

"Flynn Taggart, bring me some duct tape from the toolbox, an armload of computer-switch wiring, and the biggest goddamn boot you can find!"

He looked at me like I was crazy, but he did it. The scaffold was our ticket out of there, but first we had to get over to it. It made sense for me to go first because I weighed less. The ledge was narrow and the chains and ropes were sufficiently out of reach so that a lifeline seemed like a good idea. At least it would give me more than one chance in case I fell.

The sounds at the heavy reinforced door told me two things. First, there was one hell of an enemy out there. Second, the most powerful ones could not be in front. A hell-prince would have huffed and puffed the door down faster than a politician would grab his pension. Even a demon pinkie could have chewed his way through that door as if it was a candy bar. So the wimps were up front, and this gave us a little more time.

While Fly was collecting the stuff, we received more evidence supporting my theory. I heard screams that I'd have recognized anywhere—the noise imps make when they're being ripped apart. They were up front and not strong enough to break through. It occurred to me that this military-quality door dated back to the time of Walt Disney himself. I was glad that Disney had been a paranoid right-wing type, according to the biographies. A more trusting sort would never have installed the door that was saving our collective ass. But it wasn't going to hold much longer.

"Got it!" Fly announced, trotting back with the wire, tape, and boot. "What's your plan?"

I told him. I showed him. He nitpicked.

"I should go first because of upper male body strength and a longer reach . . ."

"I weigh less! Besides, it's my idea. You're going to be too busy to go first anyway."

He opened his mouth to ask what I meant, but the shredding of the door provided the answer. Talons appeared like little metal helmets, leaving furrows behind them as they sliced through the last barrier between us and them.

Grabbing his Sig-Cow, Fly started blasting through the door before the first one even appeared. I saw that my buddy wouldn't be able to help with the makeshift rope so I tied one end to a heavy safe and the other around my waist and clambered out the window pronto.

Luck was with me. Fly and I disagree about luck: he thinks you make your own; I think you're lucky or you're not. The ledge was so narrow that I couldn't imagine Fly negotiating it. The stupid little lifeline came apart before my hand was on one of those beautiful, thick, inviting ropes.

I shouted my patented war cry, based on all the westerns I'd seen when I was a kid, and jumped the rest of the way. I knew I'd better be right about luck.

I swung far out and heard a long creaking sound overhead, which was fine with me as long as it wasn't followed by a loud snap. Just a steady creaking, as the rope settled into supporting my weight. I didn't waste a moment swinging over to a sturdy-looking cable chain. I didn't trust the chain, so I tested it out. The damned thing snapped, and I hung over L.A. like an advertisement, glad for the rope. My left hand was covered with rust. I would have thought that the chain would outlast the rope, but maybe some of the links were caught in a random energy beam.

A lot of stuff raced through my mind. I filed most of it for future reference—if I had a future. The stuff overhead reminded me of the last time I was aboard ship—on the ocean instead of in space, I mean. The only reason I wasn't splattered all over the street below was that the window-washing equipment was securely attached on the roof. I hoped no alien energy burst had done any damage up there.

"Fly!" I yelled.

"Coming, coming, coming!" he shouted back.

There was no double entendre in either of our minds. My bud would either be a fly on the wall out here or a squashed bug inside.

He chose fly on the wall.

I made like Tarzan, or maybe I should say Sheena of the Jungle, and swung over toward the window. The scaffolding held. Fly held on. As he leaped out the window, a red claw the size of his head missed severing his jugular vein by an inch. I couldn't believe I used to feel sorry for the Minotaur trapped in the lair until Theseus came to put him out of his misery. I'd never look at those old myths the same way.

We started down. The ropes wouldn't get us to ground level, but half a loaf is better than none. If we could descend below the monsters we might have a chance to hoof it down to the street before they could catch up with us. I was counting on their habit of getting in each other's way and tearing each other up when they should have been focusing on us instead.

Fly had it tougher than I did because he was hanging like a piece of sacrificial meat directly outside the window where the enemy was massing. He was holding the rope with one hand, leaving the other free to fire repeatedly at that rectangle of horror and doom.

"Fly, I'll cover you if you climb lower," I promised. Grateful for the time I'd spent rappelling down cliffs in my high school days, I maneuvered so that the rope was wrapped around me like a lonely boa constrictor, freeing my gun hand. As I started firing thirty-caliber rounds at the window, Fly slung his weapon over his shoulder and used both hands to lower himself.

When he was safe enough—safety being relative when you're playing tag with all the denizens of hell—he yelled, "My turn to cover you!"

I made like a monkey and headed straight for certain death. Fly kept up a barrage that was truly impressive. The odds were at an all-time low, but as I made it past the window, I was ready to rethink my position on God. Fly and Albert had God. I had luck . . . and a fireball that came so close it singed my hair. Well, my high-and-tight needed a trim.

Fly ran out of rope and I joined him just in time to see his very special expression, the one he only wears when Options 'R Us has closed its doors permanently.

I couldn't help myself. I looked up. There is no mistaking a fire eater. And this one was getting ready to fry everything it could see.

The only hope was to break one of the windows, get inside the building quicker than a thought, and then haul ass down to the street. We had one chance. Fortunately we'd brought along that really big boot.

"Aw, gimme a break, you two," begged Mulligan, thoroughly beaten. "I don't care how you escaped from the tower. It's none of my business. I'll never ask again."

He threw the remaining beers at Fly and me as if they were grenades. The way the brews were shaken up, they might as well have been.

While I pointed mine at the broad expanse of the Pacific Ocean and fired off the white spray, Mulligan changed his tone. He didn't sound like a wily old master gun. He didn't even sound like a marine. He sounded like a Boy Scout trying to requisition a last piece of candy.

"Okay," I said. "I'll tell you the rest, from the point where Fly and I have no disagreements about what happened."

"Thank you," said our victim.

4

No sooner had Mulligan agreed to be a good boy and let me finish my story than he changed his mind. Just like a man.

"Uh, Sanders," he said.

"Yes, George?"

"How about we do it a little differently this time? I'll ask questions and you answer 'em. How's that?"

"Is that your first question?" I asked the master gun.

"Arlene," Fly addressed me with his I'm-not-worried-yet tone of voice, the one he uses right before he tells me that I've gone over the line. He has a big advantage in these situations: he seems to know where the line is.

Mulligan just sat there grinning, waiting for a better response from a mere PFC. "Okay," I said. "What do you want to know?"

"Looks like I should've brought more beer," he admitted. Fly still had some Jack Daniel's left, so he'd be feeling no pain. All I had to get me through was truth, justice, and the American way.

"When you reached ground level, you didn't have any wheels waiting for you," Mulligan said.

There's no way you could've outrun a mob of those things."

"No problem," I told him. "I hot-wired a car."

He grimaced. "Now I suppose Corporal Taggart will tell the story of how he was the one who—"

"No," Fly happily interrupted. "Arlene hot-wired the car all by herself. Can't imagine where a nice girl like her ever picked up such a specialized skill."

I gave Fly the finger and didn't even wait for Mulligan to ask what happened next. "I drove like crazy for the airport with Fly riding shotgun. I had the crazy idea I could hot-wire a plane and fly Fly out of there."

"Thanks," said Fly.

"Let me get this straight," Mulligan returned to the fray. "At that time you didn't realize the teenager was still waiting for you."

"Jill," said Fly.

"Jill," Mulligan repeated.

I enjoyed this next bit. "We'd told her in no uncertain terms that she was not to wait for us. We'd risked our lives taking down the force field so Jill could fly Albert and Ken to safety."

"So naturally she disobeyed orders," said Fly.

"You've got quite a kid there," observed the master gun with true respect for Jill. Fly and I exchanged looks.

"Jill is loyal." Fly spoke those words with dignity.

Mulligan steered the discussion back to my monologue: "So you only had to drive to the airport . . ."

"Except we didn't make it in the first car. No great loss, as it was an unexploded Pinto. Until it exploded! A hell-prince stepped right out into the middle of the street and you know what happens when they fire those green energy pulses from their wrist-launchers."

"You trade in the old model you're driving for a new one." Mulligan grinned; he was into the spirit of the thing now.

"Thanks to my superb driving skills—"

"You were weaving all over the road like a drunk on New Year's Eve," Fly interjected.

"Exactly," I agreed without missing a beat. "So we survived the surprise attack. I slammed the car into a row of garbage cans, and we wasted no time exiting the vehicle and returning fire."

"I wondered what Corporal Taggart was doing all this time," said Mulligan.

"Watching the rear," said Fly. "Perhaps you've forgotten we were being chased."

"So then what?"

"Good luck was what," I told the master gun. "An abandoned UPS truck was parked on the side of the street. We made our way over to it, simply hoping it was in working order. Well, we hit the jackpot. Inside was a gun nut's paradise, a whole shipment addressed to Ahern Enterprises."

"The bazooka," said Fly. "Don't forget to tell him about the bazooka."

Poor Mulligan ran out of beer. He was on his own now. "The hell-prince, as you call him, didn't fry your butts before you could use all this stuff?"

"Nope," I said. "His second shot missed us by a country klick."

"Then what happened?"

"We fried his butt," I recounted.

"But . . ." Mulligan started a thought and came to a dead stop. He tried again. "We all know how freakin' stupid these things are, but I'm surprised that in all your encounters the enemy never has any luck."

"I wonder about that myself sometimes," Fly admitted. "I wouldn't bet on my survival in most of these situations, but Arlene and I seem very hard to kill. That's why we're certain to be put back on a strike team."

"What helped us that time," I continued, "was that a bunch of pumpkins were in the vanguard of our pursuers."

"Oh, yeah," said Mulligan. "Your name for those crazy flying things. I remember your stories about how the pumpkins and hell-princes hate each other."

"We learned that on Deimos," Fly contributed.

"While the pumpkins and hell-prince wasted each other's time, we prepared the bazooka for the hell-prince. Between the pumpkins and us, we took him down. Which only left us with the problem of being surrounded by half a dozen deadly spheres. Fly and I used another trick that worked on Deimos: we stood back-to-back, and each of us laid down fire in a 270-degree sweep. That created the ingredients for a very large pie."

"So then you checked out the contents of the truck."

"Like I said, it was gun nut heaven. We did a quick inventory and took what was easiest to get at."

Fly remembered a grim moment. "I opened one box expecting to find ammo, but it was a case of books defending the Second Amendment. I even remember the title, *Stopping Power* by J. Neil Schulman. The stopping power I needed right then could not be provided by book pages."

"I had a moment of frustration, too," I said. "I found the shipping form. It showed that the most inaccessible box contained a number of specialized handguns, including one I'd always wanted. There simply wasn't enough time to unload the truck."

"What was the specialized gun?" asked Mulligan.

"Watch out," Fly warned him, but it was too late. The master gun had asked the question.

"It's a Super Blackhawk .357 Magnum caliber sidearm. Looks like an old western six-gun, but there the resemblance ends. The only drawback used to be that it didn't conceal well, with its nine inch barrel. But in today's world that's no problem! Who needs to conceal weapons any longer? Anyway, you can knock something over at a hundred yards with this gun, but it helps to have a scope. Best of all, the Blackhawk has a transfer bar mechanism. If you have a live round under the hammer and strike it with a heavy object, it won't discharge. Isn't that cool? But that's not all—"

"Arlene." Distantly I heard Fly's voice. "That's probably enough."

"But I haven't told him about the cylinder. It doesn't swing out so as to empty the spent shells. All you have to do is flip open the loading gate, push the ejection rod—"

"Arlene." Fly was using one of his very special tones of voice.

"Okay, okay," I surrendered. "Where was I? Well, we were checking out our little candy store, but we didn't have much time."

"So you hot-wired the truck?" Mulligan guessed.

"Hey, who's telling this story? The same good luck that provided us with a UPS weapons shipment left the key in the ignition and enough gas in the tank to get us to the airport. Who knows what happened to the driver? His ID was still on the dashboard—some poor bastard named Tymon. Maybe he was zombified and went looking for work at the post office. Anyway, we hauled ass and made it to the airport in record time."

Fly jumped back in. "Where I would have paddled Jill on her posterior, except that Arlene thought that might be misunderstood. Besides, I could only be so angry with someone who had probably saved our lives."

"The force field was still down," I continued. "I was surprised. Enough time had passed for them to put it up again, but we were not fighting the greatest brains in the universe. Ken seemed relieved that half his work was done."

"Half?" asked my burly audience.

"Sure. Ken had been busy while he waited for us to show up. He'd tapped into the system with an idea that turned out to be very helpful."

"So what was Jill doing all this time?" he asked.

"We took off. She didn't want to wait any longer, especially now that we could see imps and zombies piling into other planes so they could pursue us."

"Jesus," said Mulligan. "According to what you told me before, Jill had done okay; but it takes a lot more than not cracking up a plane to survive a dogfight."

"Jill was thinking along those lines herself," I said. "I tried to cheer her up by reminding her of the skill levels of the typical imp and zombie. As it turned out, it didn't matter. No sooner was Jill out past the shore than Ken solved the problem he'd been working on. He raised the force field just in time to swat the enemy planes out of the air like flies."

"Hey," said my best buddy.

"As a bonus, Ken hosed the password file so they wouldn't be able to lower the field and follow us. We realized we could actually relax for a while. Good practice for our time with you, George."

"Now, *that* part I believe," said the master gun.

5

"**O**utstanding mission," was Mulligan's verdict. "You two are a credit to the Corps."

"You've done all right yourself," I returned the compliment.

"Thanks, Fly," he said.

Meanwhile Arlene took a break from our company, and from the extended trip down memory lane. She ran into the surf. I shielded my eyes against the glaring sun to watch her precise movements. Nice to see her using her physical skills for fun instead of taking down demons. The ocean beckoned me, too. Mulligan gave it a pass.

As I watched Arlene's trim body darting in and out of the waves like a sleek dolphin, I marveled for the hundredth time that we were alive and together in a setting untouched by doom. After wading in a literal ocean of alien blood, I felt clean again in the cool ocean water. I discovered scratches and cuts and abrasions I didn't even know I had as the salt water caressed my body. Swimming stretched muscles that weren't often used in battle. I felt truly alive.

Arlene was as playful as a kid as she waved and challenged me to catch up with her. I obliged. Time for upper body strength and a longer reach to help me in my hour of need. I poured it on and moved so swiftly that my hand found her smooth ankle before she could get away.

My buddy, my fellow warrior who was as good a man as any other marine, had delicate little feet! Not like those of any other PFC of my acquaintance. The admiral could have slapped together a World War II poster with Arlene's picture and a caption: "This is what you're fighting for." We were soldiers in what might prove to be the last battle of the human race. But I liked a human face to remind me why I fought.

We splashed each other and played so hard that I swallowed a mouthful from Davy Jones's locker. And I kept finding excuses to touch the smooth skin of my buddy. There had been a subtle change between us after Albert came into her life, though.

I wasn't going to try to come between them. Just as I had steered clear of Arlene and Dodd, until her boyfriend unwillingly joined the zombie corps—*beast* all you can be. She and Albert both deserved whatever chance for happiness they could grab. We were marines. We didn't need to volunteer for the crazy suicide missions. We were assigned to them as a matter of course.

This vacation wasn't going to last.

Looking toward the beach, I saw that Mulligan had finished his beer and returned to HQ. He wasn't the type to sunbathe on purpose.

"What time is it?" asked Arlene, pausing only long enough to spit salt water in my direction.

I made a big deal of lifting my left arm to show off my brand-new plastalloy wristwatch, spaceproof and waterproof. I checked the time. "According to the best naval time, it's late afternoon."

"Teatime."

"Just about," I answered. "You know, it was about this time last week when they took the bandages off Albert's eyes."

"He beat them," she said, suddenly very serious, and I was with her all the way.

No damned imp with a lucky fireball had succeeded in blinding our big Mormon buddy. I was still pissed that Bill Ritch had been killed in similar circumstances on Deimos. Well, the bastards didn't have any of Albert. The L.A. mission had turned out to be a mortality-free operation. Hell, we'd even rescued Ken Estes when the man could do nothing to help himself. The docs had him sitting up in bed, wearing pajamas instead of mummy wrappings, and he could talk again. A bona fide miracle. Then it was Albert's turn.

"Fly," said Arlene, up close all of a sudden.

"Yeah?"

"You're a great guy," she said, and kissed me on the cheek. She could always surprise me.

"What brought that on?" I asked.

"You care about Albert," she said softly. "You care about Jill and Ken, too."

I shook my head. "Don't think that way," I told her. "You can't relax into—"

She put her hand over my mouth. It was her turn again: "You're not the only marine who can make command decisions. Soon the only people left in the world will have the will to sacrifice their loved ones if that's what it takes to defeat the invaders. Meanwhile, we can care for one another."

"You're not describing civilians," I said coldly.

She started swimming for the shore, but then turned back, treading water, and completed my education: "There are no civilians any longer, Fly. Every survivor is a soldier in this war."

I gave her that point. After all, she hadn't said everyone was a marine. I could accept the idea that all terrestrial life-forms had volunteered for grunt duty on the front line. The whole planet was the front line.

Floating on my back for a moment, I let Arlene's words wash over me. The heat of the sun and the cool of the water threatened me with sleep. We hadn't had very much of that in the past month. I'd always been naturally buoyant, but I wasn't going to risk taking a doze in the ocean. It would be funny if a guy who had survived spider-minds and steam demons drowned a short distance from his best buddy.

I swam to shore, where Arlene was waiting for me, pointing to something behind me. I looked around and for a moment thought she was referring to the cloud the admiral had noticed earlier, but it had vanished. She was interested in the black fin a hundred yards away from us.

"There's someone for your terrestrial army," I said. At the time I thought it was a shark.

"Do you think we'll ever get Jill to eat seafood?" she asked.

"I doubt it. Speaking of Jill, let's check up on her."

I'm lonely. I'm bored. I thought when we got to Hawaii I'd find some kids my own age. Everyone here is either an adult or a little kid. Some of them don't even call me Jill. They call me "the teenager."

At first they made a big fuss. The admiral gave me a medal. They were short on the real thing, so he used some old golf ribbon he'd won years ago, but it meant a lot to him, so I was polite. I was uncomfortable at the way everyone looked at me, but it was still kind of nice. The pisser was, no one would get off my age after that.

Except for Dr. Forrest Ackerman. He was probably crazy, but he was nice to me. "You're a genius," he kept repeating. "I prefer the company of geniuses."

He looked like Vincent Price from an old horror movie, complete with neat little mustache. I might not have remembered that movie except that the doctor considered himself a monster expert. "Let the others call them 'the enemy,'" he said, winking. "They're more comfortable with the old language. 'The enemy' refers to something human. We face principalities and powers. We're monster-fighters."

I had no idea what he meant by principalities and powers, but at least he didn't talk down to me.

There were a dozen computer jobs I could have taken now that I was a big hero; but I chose to work with Ackerman. For one thing, he'd asked me to. His research was interesting, and there was a lot I could do for him.

I didn't mind his interest in me, especially if I was going to be an assistant. But I didn't like the way he kept asking about the others. Albert, Fly, and Arlene had lots of military stuff to keep them busy. Ken was recovering in the hospital; whenever we talked, he tired out quickly.

"There is every indication that Ken is also a genius," Ackerman said, smiling.

"At least he's unwrapped."

"What do you mean?"

"I was, uh, making a joke. He looked like a mummy when we rescued him from the train. When I look at him now, I think of a . . . mummy."

"Yes, yes," he replied. "You and Ken were worth the sacrifices the others made."

"They were very brave."

"Normal specimens," he said to himself.

People who talk to themselves are overheard sometimes.

"What do you mean?" I asked.

He looked up from his clipboard and blinked at me through his heavy black-rimmed glasses. "Sorry. I'm spending too much time in the lab. I only meant that if the human race is going to survive, we must harvest all of our geniuses."

I'd been called a genius ever since I was a kid. Sometimes I got tired of it. "What's a genius?" I asked.

He had a quick answer. "Anyone who can think better than his neighbor."

"There must be a lot of geniuses, then."

He smiled. "Don't be a smart aleck or I won't show you my collection."

I'd always found it hard to shut up. "How do you know who's so smart?"

He placed a fatherly hand on my shoulder. I didn't hold that against him. He had no way of knowing I wasn't looking for a dad.

"Jill, the military keeps records. Sometimes I think it's all they're really good at doing. If your military friends had unusually high IQs or other indications of special mental attributes, we'd know."

"I thought a lot of records were lost during the invasion."

He laughed. It didn't sound as if he was enjoying a joke. "You should be a lawyer."

"No, thanks."

"This base had thorough documents on military personnel of all the services before Doom Day."

"Doom Day?"

"That's what we're calling the first day of the invasion. By the way, I notice you're trying to change the subject. You *are* a genius, Jill. You might find it interesting that your last name, Lovelace, is the same as that of Augusta Ada King Lovelace, an English mathematician who has been called the world's first computer programmer."

It was amazing how much trivia Ackerman carried in his head. While we were talking, I followed him into the largest laboratory I'd ever seen: an underground warehouse they'd allowed Dr. Ackerman to turn into his private world. Clearance was a cinch: he ran the lab.

I wanted to get him off the subject of my friends. The way he talked about them made me uncomfortable. They'd been sort of ignoring me lately. At least that was how it felt. I didn't want to be disloyal to them when I was already pissed off. I wasn't a rat.

Besides, maybe they were purposely giving me time to be alone. Arlene had said I could really be a pill when I was in one of my moods.

Well, why shouldn't I be? Albert and Arlene had a thing for each other. When they were like that they didn't want anyone else around, not even Fly. But lately Arlene was spending more time with Fly. They had this really gross brother-sister kind of thing going. When I first met them, I thought there might be something else between them. I quickly learned that was no way.

'Course I thought that might open the door for me to sort of find out if Fly would see me as anything other than a dumb kid or a computer geek. That went nowhere fast. No one can make me feel like a kid quicker than Fly Taggart.

"I don't care that civilization has almost collapsed," he told me one time when I let him see me dressing, or undressing—I forget which. "I have my own rules," he said. "My own personal code of conduct. A kid your age shouldn't even be thinking about such things. Now cut it out!" He said a lot more, but I tuned him out. Lucky for him that his personal code was exactly the same as that of other adults. He called it the "your actions" principle, or the YA rule for short.

Fly was just like all the other adults I'd known, except that he was a better shot. A full-grown man is telling me what I shouldn't be thinking about. Typical! At least Dr. Ackerman didn't do that to me. But I sure didn't want him to pump me about my marine friends. I didn't want to tell him that I think Fly would rather fire a plasma rifle than make love to anyone. My opinion's none of Ackerman's business.

I didn't want the doc to know that I'd rather be a scientist than a marine. That's probably no big secret. I don't want ever, ever, ever to be a marine. I hate the haircuts.

6

"**Y**ou'll find this fascinating, Jill," Dr. Ackerman promised as he led me to a massive table covered by a gigantic plastic sheet. About the only thing missing was an electrical machine buzzing and zapping from one of the old movies.

"There are too many of them to be defeated by firepower!" He sounded like the president of the Council of Twelve from the Mormon compound. But he didn't go on to talk about the power of prayer. "After what your friends told us, we must face the reality of an unlimited number of these creatures. The bio-vats witnessed by Taggart and Sanders—"

"That was before I met them."

"Yes, we were briefed, you know. They saw those vats in space—on Deimos, to be exact. The aliens can replace their creatures indefinitely, and they keep improving their models. So . . ." Ackerman had a great sense of the theatrical, playing for an audience that was only me. Reminding me of a stage magician, he reached out with both hands and yanked the big sheet off the thing on the table.

Large pieces of steam demon were spread out on a

heavy slab. The table had to be very strong to support the weight. "It's not rotting?" I said, blurting out the first words that came into my head.

"They don't decay naturally. The zombies decompose, of course, because of their original human tissue." He slipped a pair of surgical gloves on and prodded the red side of the big chest lying there all by itself. It looked like the world's biggest piece of partially chewed bubble gum.

"There's no smell," I volunteered.

"No odor, right. Not with a cyberdemon."

"A what?"

"I forgot. You call them something else, don't you?"

"Steam demons."

"Yes, well, we're standardizing the terminology for official government science. Now take the cacodemons, for instance."

"A what?"

"You call them pumpkins. I confess I like that name myself, what with the Halloween associations, but it won't do for an official name."

"Do you have any cacodemons here?"

He shook his head. "They dissolve shortly after the tissues are disrupted. When we try to secure samples for analysis, we're left with only a test tube of liquid and powder. So tell me, Jill, what do you make of the cyber . . . er, the steam demon?"

"The name 'cyberdemon' makes sense," I agreed. I didn't tell him what I thought of "cacodemon." "The mechanical parts stick into the body so deep—"

"They are not attachments," he corrected. "Look!" He pointed at the portion of the arm that began in flesh and ended in the metal of a rocket launcher.

"Neither the arm nor the launcher is complete, but the cross section shows the point of connection between the arm and the weapon. You see it, don't you, Jill? You don't need a microscope."

The only other time I'd been this close to a piece of monster was when the foot of a spider-mind almost crushed me on the train when we rescued Ken. I wondered what Ackerman called the spider-minds. Anyway, seeing a cross section of a demon was a new experience. "I don't believe it," I admitted.

"Seeing is believing."

The red shaded into silver-gray. There was no dividing line. The rocket launcher grew out of the flesh.

"That's one for Ripley," he said.

"Huh?"

"A little before your time. It means it's hard to believe, but the evidence is right before you. When I first started studying these creatures, I was most puzzled about their weapons. Think about it. The imps fire a weapon that's purely organic in nature."

"We call them imps, too. Well, sometimes spinies."

"Uh-huh. Your pumpkins do the same with their balls of concentrated acid and combustible gas. Why, then, do these larger creatures use weapons similar to the artillery used by humans?"

I'd never thought about that. If someone is trying to stab me with a switchblade, I don't wonder how he got it.

It was Dr. Ackerman's job to wonder. "All these military weapons seemed inappropriate," he went on. "If they internally create bolts of force and can project them, why develop appendages that require external ammunition?"

"I get it," I said, excited. "It's like if you're Godzilla, what do you need with a gun?"

"Perfect, Jill. You really are a smart kid."

I didn't want compliments. I wanted to keep the discussion moving. "Are you sure they get their bullets and rockets from somewhere else? Maybe they grow them, too?"

Ackerman stopped what he was doing—bringing up a computer display showing the monster's autopsy report—and took his glasses off. He pointed at me with them. "Right there you prove yourself worth more than the people I've been working with. You can help me, uh, interface with Ken, too. His doctor says it will be a while before he gets back to normal, but he's been so close to the problem that he understands aspects of their biotechnology that no one else comprehends."

I nodded. "Now I remember. Ken told us how the rockets and guns and stuff were probably first stolen from subject races. So if the gun is a separate thing, then it's not grown by a demon."

Ackerman finished my thought: "But if it's attached, then it's grown somehow. The original version of the weapon must have been stolen first. Then they modified it into their biotech."

He turned his back to me again and I noticed little red and yellow stains all over it. I didn't want to know what they were. Now he was excited as he said, "What we need is a living specimen of one of the big ones."

He grinned. Maybe he really was a mad scientist. I had to ask the obvious question: "Would you be able to control it?"

"We already handle the living zombies we have here. That sounds funny, doesn't it? Living zombies."

"You have live ones?" I nearly freaked when he said that. Being in combat had turned me into a killer . . . of the undead.

"Sure, but they're easy to control. They don't have superhuman strength. You know that from fighting them."

"Have you fought them?"

"Well, no, but I've studied them."

"Trust me on this, Doctor—they're dangerous."

"But manageable. That's all I'm saying. If we had a live cyberdemon, then we'd have a problem of containment. The same as if our mancubus was living. I know you call them fatties."

"You have a whole fatty?"

"Fortunately it's dead. Unlike the specimen here, he seems to be slowly decaying."

I laughed. "They smell so bad alive I don't see how they could get any worse."

"The stench reminds me of rotting fish, sour grapes, and old locker-room sweat. Come on. I'll show you." He didn't need to take my arm, but I let him. He was like a friendly uncle who wanted to show off his chamber of horrors. We went past sections of flying skulls laid out like bikers' helmets. I'd always wanted a motorcycle.

"What do you call the Clydes?"

"We don't," he answered quickly. "We think your friends were wrong to think they might be the product of genetic engineering. They're probably the human traitors who were given some kind of treatment to make them tractable."

The fatty was behind glass and made me think of a gigantic meat loaf that had been left out in the sun. The metal guns it used for arms had been removed and stacked up next to the monster like giant flash-lights. He looked sort of pathetic without them.

"You can't smell it from here, but if you want to step into the room . . ."

"No, thanks." I turned him down, unsure if he was kidding me. "Let's see the zombies."

I wish I hadn't asked.

He led me to the end of the warehouse, where I finally saw some other people in white lab coats. For a moment it had seemed as if the whole place belonged to Ackerman and his monsters. We went out into a corridor. I figured the zombies had been given a special place of their own.

Like I said, what's great about scientists is the way they refuse to talk down to kids. Ackerman started to lecture, and it was fine with me:

"The most interesting part about studying zombies is the residual speech pattern. We have recorded many hours of zombie dialogue. Some of them fixate on the invasion, speaking cryptically about gateways and greater forces that lie behind them. Others pick up a pattern from their own lives, repeating phrases that tell us something about them. A final test group doesn't speak at all. We are attempting to find out if they retain any capacity to reason after the transformation."

"No," I said as strongly as I could. "The human part of them is dead."

"I understand how you must feel," he said. "It's easier for all of us if we assume we're not killing anyone human on the other end of the gun barrel."

I shook my head. "You don't understand," I told him. "I'll kill any skag who betrayed us. The traitors are still human. I wouldn't have any problem pulling the trigger on those creeps in the government who helped the demons."

"All right, calm down," he said in a completely different tone of voice. "I was really talking about myself just then. It's easier for me to work on these, er, zombies, if I think there's no humanity left."

Arlene keeps saying I can be a real pill, so I decided to be that way on purpose. I asked, "What difference does that make to you, Doctor, if they weren't geniuses when they were alive?"

He laughed instead of getting mad. "You *are* smart, Jill. I need to watch my step around you. I hope we'll enjoy working together. We can start now. What's your theory of why a few of the big monsters seem able to reason?"

"You mean like the spider-minds?"

I didn't need to tell him what that word meant. "Apparently all of them. Then there was the loquacious imp whom Corporal Taggart reported encountering on Phobos."

He was on one of my favorite subjects. "We wondered about the smart ones when we were doing the L.A. mission."

"What were your conclusions?"

I suddenly noticed how long we'd been walking. "How much farther before we reach the zombies?"

"Not long. Just don't ask if we're there yet! It'll make me think of you as a kid again."

"Is there a rest room I can use?"

"Just a few feet beyond the zombie pen." He sounded impatient. "So what did all of you conclude?"

"Whenever a normal, stupid one talks, there must be a smarter one somewhere, sending the words."

"Like broadcasting a radio signal. We've been

working along the same lines. Do you think the spider-minds do their own thinking?"

"Search me."

"They could be on the receiving end as well."

"So tell me about your zombies." I was truly interested. We'd walked a good distance and still no sight of the corpse-creeps.

"Well, we have a total of thirteen. We've run identity checks. You know how impossible it is to destroy information today."

"Yeah, the monsters can't rip a big hole in the Net, even with their fat asses."

"They've slowed us down, but they can't stop us cold."

"We'll stop them cold."

"Attagirl! Anyway, one of the zombies was once an editor named Anders Monsen. He repeats phrases from his profession. At least, that's what we think he's doing. One of the women is Michelle DeLude, a blonde. She keeps repeating how she must get to Las Vegas in time for her wedding. Mark Stephens ran a bookstore. Butler Shaffer was a law professor. Tina Karos was a paralegal. She's the brunette. Both the ladies were very attractive in life. Shame to see them monsterized. The other eight were seamen stationed right here in Hawaii. One was a huge man his friends called Big Lee. Don't remember the names of the others."

Ackerman could have been a teacher. He made me want to meet his special class of dead people. I was looking forward to it . . . until the door marked Maximum Security swung open and a large shape filled the doorway, swinging a meat cleaver with which it hacked off Dr. Ackerman's head.

7

I'll never admit this to Arlene, but for the first time I doubt my faith. I don't want to be Albert the agnostic. I have to write this out of my system. When I'm finished, I'll destroy it and write her a real letter. It might seem stupid to write to someone I could speak to in person, but when I look into her green eyes, I become tongue-tied. The way she arches her right eyebrow and smiles with a smile as hot as her flaming red hair, I just can't talk to her. She offers me herself, and all I can do is tell her about my religion.

She was the first sight I beheld after the operation. They did what they could for my face, but I didn't need to look in a mirror to realize I had permanent scars. My face still burns. It will burn forever from the new valleys and ridges etched into my forehead and cheeks and chin. I suppose there is consolation in not being as ugly as an imp. Of course, I'll have a head start if I'm ever turned into a zombie.

I know it's wrong to worry about my appearance when I could have been blind for the rest of my life. May God forgive my vanity.

Arlene won't let me be sorry for myself. She bent over my hospital bed, smiling like an angel, and kissed up and down the tortured flesh of my disfigured face. "You'll always be my Albert," she whispered so that only I could hear.

We've shared experiences few mortals will ever know. We've faced down the wrath of a spider-mind. We've tasted the brimstone of a fire eater. (I can't figure out why the scientists here call those things arch-viles.) Together we've spilled the slimy guts of pumpkins and princes of hell. I was willing to wade through a sea of blood with this woman. But when she turned her face to me and offered me her high cheekbones to touch and her full mouth to kiss, I pulled away.

She must think I'm a fool. A woman who has proved herself in a world of men, she is not squeamish about the human body. Women tend to be more matter-of-fact about the body anyway. They already live in the sea of blood so it must seem very strange to watch men deliberately embark upon that crimson ocean. Does a foxhole really compare to childbirth? I was brought up to believe that the highest destiny of a woman is to bring children into the world. The church reinforced these attitudes. I can respect a woman who is a fighter but I can't shake the idea she's shirking her responsibility as a woman. It's like if she dies on a battlefield, she gets off easy. If she's an officer, she exercises a trivial kind of authority compared to what God intends for her to do with her children.

So here comes Arlene Sanders with her high-and-tight, tossing back her head as if she had long hair down to her waist, showing off her long neck and firm jaw, and shouldering her piece with as much authority as any man. Yeah, I'll pretend it's the day after Halloween and help her blow away pumpkins. But I won't touch her with my naked hand.

Intellectually, I don't doubt the Book of Mormon.
History shows that a life of marriage and children is
intended for men and women on this earth. When we
move away from that, we become miserable. When we
do our duty, we know a happiness of which no
hedonist can even dream.

I guess my problem is that I thought I'd been
tempted before. But the women who offered themselves to me for quick and easy sex were not women I
respected. They'd never stood up to devils from the
depths of space. They'd never encountered the now-
or-never choice of giving up your life for a buddy—
and surviving only because he'd do the same for you.
I'd met plenty of women who were into rock, but PFC
Arlene Sanders was the first who could really rock and
roll!

Turning down her offer hurts so much because if a
buddy asked for anything else, I'd come through
without giving it a second thought. How can she treat
the act of love so casually? I know lots of men who'd
jump at the chance offered by Arlene, but she probably wouldn't be interested in them. My usual lousy
luck—she's attracted to me because she knows I'll say
no.

Even when I was a jock back in high school, there
were cheerleaders after me. Being big and muscular
has its advantages. The smart guys thought I was
stupid and left me alone. That was probably an
advantage also.

I want a family. I want a loving wife who will give
me children. It's that simple, but I can't make the
words come out. Words are fragile tools. When you
try to turn them into weapons they often break. I can't
write the letter to Arlene today. I don't have the

words. I pray that I'll find the words while we're still together.

In a world of real demons, there isn't any time to waste. Nor is this a good time to question my faith just because I suddenly discover I cannot govern my passions. I might even have a future in which to raise a family.

Once, when I was reading a book in the Mormon library, I came across a line that stayed with me. I don't remember the author, but he said: "Happy families are all alike; every unhappy family is unhappy in its own way." I take that to mean that happiness grows out of love. Love is based on your actions. So is faith.

How do I tell Arlene that I want all or nothing? Especially when she's already offered me more than I deserve . . . And how can we make a decision for the future in a world like this? My hell on Earth is a world where Arlene is right and I'm wrong. Do we even have a right to try to plan for the future? If we were the last two people in a universe of monsters, there would be a certain legitimacy in trying to make a life together, in however brief a span was allotted to us. But our lives are not our own. There is the Corps. One, two, three, four, *she* loves the Marine Corps. She loves it more than I do. So does Fly. There is that link between them.

We are under orders more severe than any monastery could impose. Perversely, I have taken an oath of celibacy that she has not taken. Arlene Sanders is a worldly woman, whether on this planet or off.

But I am honest enough to admit that I have no intention of changing. If it were proven to me tomorrow that the Mormon faith is false, I would not become a moral relativist. I would not treat human relations as casual affairs. I take people too seriously for that. I'd still believe in my morality even if no God provided supernatural guidance.

I pray that one day Arlene will understand how much faith I have in her. Suddenly I realize that I can't write her a letter. I have to tell her all this in person. Despite all my reservations, I must have the courage of my convictions.

I'm going to ask her to marry me.

"Arlene, look out!"

The little voice in the back of my head just wouldn't shut up about how stupid it was to go anywhere without being armed to the teeth. Arlene and I hadn't felt safe enough to go unarmed since the first day of the Phobos invasion. We even kidded each other about going to the beach without either of us packing a piece. I wouldn't have minded seeing her with a nice Colt .45 strapped to her and leaving its mark on her nearly naked body. She's my buddy, but I still have an imagination.

Here we were in a stronghold of humanity. This was one place where we didn't have to feel like the black gang-banger surrounded by white cops in what a police commissioner might refer to as a target-rich environment. Here we could let down our hair—a joke when you have a marine haircut—and go naked, which has nothing to do with clothes and everything to do with being unarmed.

Nothing threatened us on the beach, except maybe that lazy shark we'd noticed right before coming in. We didn't have any need of firepower when we went through the security check. We simply needed our big bath towels because the air conditioning was on full blast inside. It was still our day of R&R, and neither of us was in a rush to get back into uniform. I'd never enjoyed wearing civvies more in my life.

We weren't expecting trouble as we went looking for Jill. Ackerman's monster lab was a lot closer than Albert, who'd "gone to town," and Arlene figured her beau still needed time alone.

It wasn't until we went into the biology research department that the old marine training kicked in. Something just didn't feel right. Maybe it was not seeing more people than we did. But when I noticed the female lab technician from behind, I knew something was wrong. Her long black tresses were a tattered mass stained with splotches of green. She had a great figure, and something told me she'd never let her hair go like that. Her lab coat was wrinkled and disgustingly dirty, though I knew the admiral ran a tight ship and wouldn't abide slovenliness.

Arlene picked up the pace and started hoofing it over to the technician. As the woman started to turn, I couldn't believe that Arlene wouldn't notice the messy hair and the dirty lab coat. My best buddy wasn't just a great warrior; she was female.

No sooner did I shout, "Arlene, look out," than I realized I didn't need to worry about her. She went into a roll that made her a less promising target than I was. Marine, protect your own ass!

Turning sideways, I flattened myself against the wall before the female zombie got off her first shot. Arlene made certain she didn't get another. Zombie reflexes suck. Even a woman in good physical condition would have had trouble stopping Arlene coming up from the floor, right arm straight up like the Statue of Liberty, and knocking the gun from the cold leathery hand that was yet to get off a second shot.

The next few seconds proved to be the corollary to "Practice Makes Perfect." We'd both become a little rusty. There was no other explanation for Zombie Girl getting away before Arlene could slam her hard against the convenient back wall—providing plenty of time for one of us to retrieve the gun from the floor and pump lead into the leathery blue-gray face of our walking beauty.

This zombie lass moved very quickly, though—faster than any zombie I'd ever seen. She also shouted something very strange about having to get to court. Then she darted through a door to my left before Arlene could reach her from the rear or I could approach her from the front.

"Those morons!" Arlene screamed. "What kind of security do they call this?"

I was pissed too, but I had more sympathy for a genuine blunder than Arlene did. Watching that bastard Weems order the murder of the monks in Kefiristan had softened me toward mere incompetence. The science boys had to study everything they could get their hands on. I didn't expect there wouldn't be risks. But whatever had gone wrong, it was now a job for people like Arlene and me.

She'd already picked up the piece from the floor, a .38 caliber revolver. I liked the idea of acquiring more artillery as quickly as possible.

A scream from the other side of the door brought us back to immediate reality. Reconnoitering was a luxury, and going to the armory was a vacation from the job.

We went through the door together, me coming in low and Arlene braced, pointing the gun ahead of us—a beacon of truth with its own special kind of flame. But she didn't fire right away. She was afraid of hitting the woman that the zombie in the lab coat was carving up like a Christmas turkey.

The victim stared at us without seeing what was in front of her. The broken beaker in the zombie's hand occupied the woman's full attention. Zombie Girl had already cut her victim around her breasts and arms. The angle made it impossible for us to alter the events of the next few seconds. That was all the time the zombie needed.

She drew her makeshift knife in a slashing movement across the white throat of the victim. The throat didn't stay white very long. The lifeblood spurted out so fast that it covered the hand holding the broken glass, and it looked as if the zombie had spilled a bucket of red paint over itself.

Arlene took a few lithe dancer's steps into the room and placed her gun right up against the Zombie Girl's head. This walking dead might be fast, but the jig was up. Arlene squeezed off a round. Blood, brains, and gore splattered back over the victim, but the poor woman was past caring. She was still twitching, but that didn't count. We couldn't save her.

"Too bad none of the scientists are around to observe that," I said, pointing. A piece of zombie brain continued to flop around on the floor with a life of its own. I'd noticed this phenomenon before. It seemed to apply only to the better rank of zombies, the ones with a shred of initiative left.

"She was a fast one," said Arlene, nodding at the woman we didn't save. "If I were wearing my boots, I'd grind this to pulp," she sneered at the blue-green brain matter that seemed to be trying to crawl away. She didn't step on it. Instead, she wasted ammo.

I could relate. Quick as that, we were both back in killing mode. Then we heard another scream—one we both recognized right away. Jill!

8

"**W**e've got to save her, Fly!"

Arlene had recognized our kid, too. We'd both started thinking about Jill that way—as our responsibility. We hadn't gone through all this crap just to let her die now.

"Come on!" I shouted and headed toward the sound.

When we returned to the corridor, another zombie was waiting for us, a male. This was one of the talkative ones. He didn't babble about the Gateways and the invasion. Instead, he kept repeating, "Write it over and resubmit." I didn't give him a chance to repeat his mantra. Arlene had our only gun, but I was angry at not having been in time to save the woman in the next room. Sometimes I like to get personal.

I felt the skin crawl between my shoulders as I hit the blue-gray face with my right fist. Marines were not meant to touch this reeking leather that once was human skin, but I was too angry to care. The sound of the nose cracking did my soul a world of good. Unlike Arlene's prey, this one was slow. I could have moved a lot slower, but adrenaline surged through me as I did something I'd never done to any of these bozos: I gave it the old one-two with straight fists. No karate, no fancy side kicks, no special training. I just pummeled that damned face in a sincere effort to send it straight back to hell, where it belonged.

"Fly!" Arlene was right behind me.

"Be with you in a second," I said.

"What about Jill?"

Shit. How could I have been sidetracked so easily? There are certain drawbacks to being a natural warrior. "Take it," I yelled, resuming the twenty-yard dash—thirty? forty?—to save Jill. I measured distance in *kill*-ometers. I didn't bother looking back as I heard the solid, satisfying sound of Arlene putting a round in the zombie's head.

Arlene stays in good shape. I never slowed down, but suddenly she was running right beside me. We found a dead guard slumped against the wall. Recent kill. Blood still trickling down his arm onto his M1. Dumb-ass zombies didn't relieve him of his satisfaction. I grabbed the weapon without slowing down, and then Arlene and I slammed through a pair of unlocked doors, ready for anything.

Anything consisted of a zombie ripping open a sawbones with the man's own surgical instruments. I fired off six rounds of .30-06 little round scalpels that opened up the zombie a lot more completely than he'd managed to do to the doctor.

"I can save him," said Arlene, noticing the convenient medikit at the same time I did. In Kefiristan, she'd had plenty of experience treating abdominal wounds. Before I could say diddly, she was on her knees, scooping up the medical guy's intestines and shoveling them back into the patient. Fortunately, the guy had passed out; and just as fortunately Arlene was really good at handling slippery things.

Jill was my responsibility—if it wasn't already too late to save her. As if on cue, she screamed again. I gave a silent prayer of thanks to Sister Beatrice, the toughest nun I'd had back in school. She always said the only prayers that are answered are the ones you say when you truly want to help someone else.

I humped. I hurried. I tried my damnedest to fly. . . .

Jill was still alive when I got to her. I almost tripped over the head of Dr. Ackerman, staring up at me with a really surprised expression. I did slip in the blood, and dropped the M1 as I careened right into the back of the biggest freakin' zombie I'd ever seen. The creep had cornered Jill and was trying to get at her with a blasted meat cleaver. She was holding him off with a metal chair, like a lion tamer. She'd taken shelter in a tight corner, which gave her an advantage: he couldn't swing the cleaver in a full arc, and she was able to avoid him by sidestepping the blade.

I slammed hard into the back of her lion, and he fell forward. Jill jumped out of the way and shouted, "Fly!" That was all, just my name, but she crammed so much gratitude into that one syllable she made me feel like the cavalry, Superman, and Zorro all rolled into one.

"Run!" I shouted, now that she had a clear escape route.

"No way!"

The brat liked giving me lip. It was hard to be mad at her though, because she was trying to retrieve the weapon from the floor. The big, hulking zombie was slow, but he didn't seem interested in giving us all the time in the world.

Jill leveled the M-1 at our problem and pulled the trigger. *Nada.* Either Jill was doing something wrong or the gun had jammed. Zombie was still fixated on her, even though I was behind him again. Jill looked at me with a hurt-little-girl expression as if to say *I gave up a perfectly good metal chair for a gun that doesn't fire?*

The bad guy still had his cleaver, and he had plenty of elbow room now, so he could swing the thing and add Jill's head to his collection. It pissed me off that all my heroics had only made Jill's situation worse. I did what I could. The big hulk was standing with his feet just far enough apart so that I was able to kick him in the groin. I wished I had on my combat boots instead of sneakers. I wished he were alive, as the dead ones are only mildly bothered by that kind of action. But it was the best I could manage.

The big bearded mother turned his head. That was all Jill needed. She held the barrel in both hands and swung the weapon so fair and true that it was worthy of the World Series. The wooden stock cracked against the zombie's neck. He was thrown off-balance. As he tried to turn his head, I heard a snap: Jill had done something bad to his old neck bone. Good girl!

The zombie fell to his knees. Before he could get out of his crouch I karate-chopped the back of his neck. No time to play George Foreman now. So far, Jill and I had merely slowed him down. Time for something more permanent.

Jill had the same idea. No sooner did I body-slam the hulk into a prone position than she yanked the cleaver away from him and started swinging it at his head.

"Hey, watch it!" I shouted. "You almost hit me."

"Sorry," she said, almost as a gasp. But she kept swinging that wicked blade at the peeling, rotten flesh around the zombie's neck and head. I wasn't about to tell her she didn't have the strength to finish the job. The zombie wasn't getting up, and I intended to make sure it stayed down.

As I retrieved the M1, I realized that no other zombies were showing up to bother us. There was something eerie about Doc Ackerman's head on the floor, staring at us. (A marine isn't supposed to use a word like "eerie," but it *was* freakin' eerie, man.)

I picked up the M1. So it had jammed for Jill. So she'd used it as a club. It's not like she'd smashed it against a tree. I cleared the bolt. What the hell, we'd give it another try.

"Excuse me," I said to Jill, busily trying to return the favor to the great decapitator. The meat cleaver was a little dull. And Jill just didn't have the necessary body mass. She offered me her hatchet. I declined.

I fired the M1 once, point-blank. The head came apart like a ripe cantaloupe. The blood that poured out was a brand-new color on me.

"The gun jammed," she insisted.

"I know."

"I didn't do anything wrong with it!"

"I'm not saying you did. Knocking the gun around probably unjammed it."

"Well, I just want you to know it wasn't my fault that I couldn't fire it."

There were times when Jill went out of her way to remind me she was a teenager. I really wasn't in the mood for her defensiveness just then. God knew how many more zombies were roaming the installation. We had to get back to Arlene. And I was worried about Albert. We'd become like a family.

At some moment in my military career I'd become used to the stench of death. I could probably thank the Scythe of Glory and their Shining Path buddies for that. But I would never get used to the sour-lemon zombie odor; and the strongest whiff of it I'd had in a very long time scorched my nostrils as the head of the dead zombie leaked at my feet.

When I threw up, I knew the vacation was over.

I am Ken. I once was part of a family. They're all dead now. I once took long walks every day and rode a bicycle. I swam. I ate food off plates and drank wine. I sang. I made love.

Now I am a cybermummy. A Ken doll. They have taken off the bandages and removed some of the objects from my flesh, but I feel that the aliens have made me less than human. Dr. Ackerman thought the opposite; but I don't feel more than human. Dr. Williams, the director, says they will bring me back to normal, but I don't believe him. The director puts nothing above the importance of winning the war. I am more useful to him now where I am, remaining what I am. The medical team tries to keep its findings from me, but I can tap into all their computer systems.

They say they can overcome my physical weakness quite easily. They can stop feeding me intravenously and slowly acclimate my system to regular food again.

Simple brain surgery would restore full mobility, but there is a risk—not to me but to their project. The alien biotech in my head could be altered or lost in the course of getting me back to normal. So they take their time.

Meanwhile, I am plugged into the computers and confined to my bed, except when they risk placing me in a motorized wheelchair. I do not complain about this. I do not tell Jill when she comes to visit me. She's my most frequent visitor. I don't complain to Flynn or Arlene or Albert when they check up on me. These are the people who saved me. They care about me. I see no reason to make them worry.

Keeping my own counsel is a trick I learned when I was very young. I don't tell anyone how much I want to be the man I was. My favorite uncle used to take his family to Hawaii for vacations. He'd tell us all about it when he visited, and I wanted so much to come here. The irony is that here may be one of the last places on Earth where things are still as he remembered, and I can't go out and see them while there is still time.

I access all that I can on Hawaii. The screen flickers and tells me that Hawaii is a group of islands stretching for over three hundred miles in the middle of the Pacific Ocean. I bring up information on how it was discovered by Europeans; and then I read how it became the fiftieth state of the United States. I remember my uncle saying the most popular fish here is difficult to spell, and I find an entry for it, and I realize my uncle was an honest man: *humumunukunukuapuaa*. I read all about King Kamehameha and envy how he could get around the islands so much more easily than I . . .

I grow tired of feeling sorry for myself. I don't mind being useful. I'm not certain that's the same thing as doing one's duty, but I don't really care. This could be the last stand of the human race. But I hate the lies. All the military is good at doing in a crisis is lying. I would never talk about this with brave soldiers. They don't want to hear about it. There is no point in discussing it with cynical senior officers, especially those who have decided to use me without being honest about their intent.

I like my new friends. They have honor. They look out on the world with a clean vision that no amount of dirt or blood can obstruct. They think they are fighting for individualism. For freedom. If the human race survives, they will face a serious disappointment. I have accessed the files. There are plans.

Perhaps I am closer to the future than those who rescued me. I am trapped inside myself. Maybe something deep inside me died when I was in the clutches of the invaders. Before they altered me, I would have been horrified to discover human plans for a New Eugenics to build the future. This is not a plan of the human collaborators. The traitors have their own genetic plans for "improving" that part of humanity the new masters will allow to survive.

The New Eugenics is a plan devised by *our* side. The good guys. The ones fighting the invaders. Who knows? Maybe they will deliberately create more computer adjuncts like me! It's a dead certainty that they will begin making breeding decisions for the survivors on our side. Warriors like Flynn and Arlene will be spared this nonsense. They were born to die in battle. They are too valuable to use in non-military operations. I have accessed plans for them. They don't know it yet, but their time on Earth is limited. Very few people have their skill as space warriors. Flynn is Flash Gordon. Who is Arlene? Barbarella?

Marines Taggart and Sanders will follow orders even when it involves facing hundred-to-one odds and near-certain death. I'd like to imagine some bureaucrat, human or otherwise, telling them with whom they should go to bed and how many children they are expected to have. They will be spared this future Earth that I believe to be inevitable, no matter which side wins. Times of crisis are made in hell—and made for the kind of man who has a plan for everything.

Jill and I are to remain on Earth! If Albert is fortunate, he will go with Fly and Arlene. He is too religious a man to stay. Where would he turn when he found out there's no side for him? Would he try to return to Utah? He doesn't know about Utah yet. He'll probably find out today.

They have a lot to cover today. The service for Ackerman and his staff was held this morning. I watched it on the monitor. So much has happened since yesterday.

First, the admiral will pretend there was a possibility of sabotage even though the video recordings show that the killings were the result of simple carelessness on the part of one of Ackerman's staff. Plain incompetence led to the holocaust. Those tapes remain classified, naturally. The possibility of a traitor does more for gung-ho morale than an admission of incompetence. I can hardly fault our new leaders for being students of history.

Besides, my friends will be receiving a big dose of declassified material relevant to their next mission.

They shouldn't be greedy for too much declassified material all at once. It causes indigestion. Besides, their marine colonel will be giving them a nice dessert.

I should have a better attitude about this. The other side is so terrible that we should forgive our own shortcomings. Isn't that what they said when they were fighting Hitler? The doom demons, as Jill likes to call them, are perfect enemies. In the name of fighting them, we can do anything we want. No, it isn't fair to say we want to do terrible things. We will win by any means necessary, as Malcolm X used to say.

9

By the time I joined Fly and Jill, I could breathe easy again. It was Fly *and* Jill. He saved her. I knew the big lug would. There was no way I could have left a man bleeding to death when I had the training to save him.

Of course, the navy's security forces were swarming everywhere by then. I didn't mind that two of the first of Kimmel's finest were Mark Stanfill and Jim Ivey, my poker playing buddies (Fly wasn't in our league).

When everything's gone to hell in a hand basket, personal ID can make the crucial difference in whether somebody panics and pulls the trigger. Ackerman's facilities had been turned into a zombie cafeteria, and that was enough to make anyone panic.

Fly, Jill, and I were hustled into a decontamination chamber. After all the contact we'd had with these creatures I almost laughed at precautions this late in the game. Then again, I shouldn't criticize Hawaii Base for being thorough. It would be a kick in the ass if we defeated the enemy only to succumb to diseases already coursing through our bloodstreams.

In the evening, I saw Albert at dinner. He was a worse poker player than Fly because he couldn't keep emotions from marching across his face.

"Arlene, are you all right?" he asked, noticing Jill's smile a second later. "Are *all* of you okay?" he added.

"We're fine," Fly assured him, grinning.

"We needed the practice," Jill added.

"Stop giving him a hard time," I told the other two. "Don't mind these kill-crazy kids, Albert."

"Hey!" Fly protested, still smiling.

"Seriously, Albert, after all we've done together, this was no big deal." I noticed that other tables frequently occupied by now were only half full. The death toll hadn't been that high, considering the surprise element. All the zombies were accounted for, and wasted. (At least Ackerman kept good records.) The only explanation for the sparse crowd was that a number of our comrades had been put off their food by a first sloppy encounter with the drool ghouls. So we could have seconds if we wanted.

Albert sighed and joined us. The tables were set up cafeteria-style, and our little group tended to gravitate together. We were so taken with Ken that he'd probably belong to our little supper club if he ever ate solids again.

"I didn't hear about the zombies until I returned," he said almost apologetically.

"How was town?" asked Jill.

"I was shopping." Those innocuous words came out of Albert freighted with an extra meaning. I wasn't the only one who heard it.

We ate our Salisbury steaks in silence. I finished and started to get up with the intention of depositing my tray in the proper receptacle. I figured my figure didn't really need the extra calories of seconds, after all. Albert was only starting to eat, but he abandoned his food. And Albert is a growing boy.

"Do you mind if I walk with you?" he asked. The style was definitely not him. I couldn't help noticing Jill's eyes burning into him. She sensed something was up. Fly was busy paying close attention to his pineapple dessert.

"Sure," I said. For one moment I let wishful thinking override the rational part of my brain. I wanted to believe that Albert had changed his mind about our sleeping together. I'd forgotten that where this big, wonderful guy was concerned, the most important aspect of sleeping together was the dreaming that went along with it—and the promises.

I don't know what surprised me more. That he'd come up with a ring during his shopping expedition, or that he put it to me with such direct simplicity: "Arlene, will you marry me?"

I'd opened the door to this when I made a play for him. If I had a half a brain, I'd have realized what my interest would mean to a man of this caliber.

We stood together next to a perfect facsimile of a World War II era poster proclaiming, "Loose lips sink ships." He watched me closely, especially my mouth, waiting for words promising his own personal salvation or damnation. I'd have been happier if he'd looked away. Suddenly I wasn't as brave as I thought I was.

"Albert." I only got the one word out. His expression spoke volumes. He'd certainly wrestled with all the problems haunting me. I wouldn't even insult him by bringing them up.

"That ring . . ." he began.

"It's beautiful, but I couldn't dream of accepting it until . . . I mean, I need to think . . ."

It was like one of those comedies where the characters talk at cross-purposes. Who would think a simple gold band could present a greater challenge than escaping from the Disney Tower?

"I'd like you to keep it," he said. "You don't have to think of it as an engagement ring, or anything you don't want it to be. I don't expect you to wear it, if you're not sure. Arlene, you mean so much to me that when you offered what I couldn't accept, I had to respond in my own way. I had to let you know how I feel."

Reaching out to take his hand was the easiest thing in the world, until I felt the slight tremor in his palm. It took all my courage to gaze into his eyes and say, "I can't tell you now. You must understand."

"Of course I do."

"Thank you," I said and kissed him on the cheek. His smile was a more beautiful sight than any golden ring could ever be. "I'd like to have this," I continued. "Is that right, I mean, before I . . ."

He was too much of a gentleman to let me finish. "I'd be honored if you keep it, Arlene, whatever you decide. We need to get used to making our own rules in our brave new world."

This was unexpected talk from my big, fine Mormon. "Does your God approve of that kind of thinking?" I asked him.

He took my challenge in stride. "If those of my faith are right, Arlene, he's everybody's God, isn't he?" Then he returned my chaste kiss and left me to my own devices.

The next morning, at the briefing for everyone with a Level 5 clearance or higher, I proudly wore the thin band of gold on the chain with my dog tags. Fly noticed it right away. I'll bet he was as glad as I was to be back in uniform.

Admiral Kimmel wore the face any CO puts on when the situation is grave. So did the highest-ranking officer the Marine Corps had in Hawaii, Colonel Dan Hooker. When these men were officiating together, the situation was plenty serious.

"We are investigating the possibility of sabotage," said the admiral. "Fortunately, quick thinking on the part of men and women who weren't asleep at the switch kept our losses low and neutralized the zombie threat. The navy is grateful for the help we received from marine personnel."

The two officers shook hands. The way these men regarded each other, they put more into that handshake than plenty of salutes I've seen in my day. It was nice having officers who paid attention to details. The same could be said of the man Admiral Kimmel introduced next.

Professor Warren Williams was in charge of all the

scientific work being done in Hawaii. It was difficult to pinpoint his area of greatest expertise. He had degrees in physics, astronomy, biology, computer science, and folklore. His motto was taken from the science fiction writer, Robert A. Heinlein: "Specialization is for insects."

He had a sense of humor, too, which he now demonstrated. "In his copious spare time, the admiral explains military terminology to me. I thought 'mission creep' is what we had yesterday when those creeps got loose in Ackerman's lab." He earned only a few nervous chuckles for that quip. The memory of the dead was still too fresh.

He changed the subject: "In normal times my position would be held only by someone with a certain degree of military training. A year ago I would have described myself as a militant civilian." This won him a few more chuckles. "Not since World War II have so many ill-prepared eggheads been thrown into the military omelet. But when there's no choice, there's no choice. I may have taken my first step toward this job when I first learned about the top secret of the Martian moons. I was suspicious of the Gates the moment I realized that anything might come through them."

He looked a little like Robert Oppenheimer. I could imagine him working on the A-bomb. "The admiral and I agree on how you can tell when you are in perilous times. That's when people go out of their way to listen to the advice of engineers." Only one person laughed at this. Me.

He covered other material about the operations of the base, but his eyes kept coming to me. I didn't think he was going to ask for a date. Fly and I had proved ourselves too often, too well. I figured we were first choice for the director's punch line; and we'd better not have a glass jaw.

He proved me right when the general briefing was over and he asked to see the Big Four, as we sometimes jokingly called ourselves. I'm sure there were adults at the base who resented a kid like Jill being entrusted with material that was off-limits to them. But if so, they kept it to themselves.

Jill's growing up fast. There's nothing wrong with that. I know it bugs Fly when men old enough to be her father start giving her the eye. She's tall for her age. She has one of those pouty mouths that drive men nuts. I don't worry about who kisses that mouth so long as the brain directly over it is in charge. In between spilling demon guts all over the great American West, I took Jill aside and gave her the crash course in birds, bees, and babies.

Of course, she doesn't have to worry about any sexually transmitted diseases. Medical science marches on. But who would have thought that no sooner does the human race eliminate AIDS than along come monsters from space? In the words of the late-twentieth-century comic, Gilda Radner, "It's always something."

Anyway, Fly acts more and more like a worried father where Jill is concerned. This can be a good thing. It gave him that extra bit of fire when he saved her in Ackerman's lab. But I don't know how to tell him to let go when I can't solve my own personal problems—Albert as a prospective husband.

Albert is a sensitive man, a shy man. I don't want to hurt him. I'd rather eat one of my own mini-rockets than make him suffer. But I've spent my life being true to *myself.* Now I don't know if it's concern for Albert that makes me hesitate to accept his marriage proposal . . . or if I fear commitment to a man I love more than I do a roomful of lost souls, the dumb name the science boys have given the flying skulls. If I survive our final missions, and Earth is secure once more, will I be willing to give this man children? I don't even want to think about it. Yet I know that that expectation is implicit in his proposal. To Albert, marriage without trying to have children only counts as serious dating. Maybe I'm afraid of asking Fly to be godfather to my kids.

As the director led us into his inner sanctum, I felt once again that the four of us had already formed a strange family unit of our own. Maybe we were the model of the smallest functional social unit of the future—but make sure the kid has a good aim!

As I gazed at the gigantic radio-controlled tele-scope, the long tube reminded me of a cannon, a perfect symbol for combining the scientific and the military. Williams stood in front of it, feet braced, hands behind his back. He seemed more military at that moment than the admiral and the colonel, who stood over to the side, as if deferring to the scientist.

Before the director even opened his mouth I had the sinking feeling that all our personal problems were about to be put on the back burner. Again.

10

"**C**orporal Taggart," the director addressed me. "How did you like your time in space?"

I'm always honest when no life is at stake. "I always wanted to go, sir. If you know my record, you're aware I didn't get up there in the way I intended."

"If ever a court-martial was a miscarriage of justice, yours would've been," volunteered Colonel Hooker, looking directly at me. "One good thing about wartime is that it makes it easy to cut through the red tape. I enjoyed pencil-whipping that problem for you, marine!"

"Thank you, sir."

The director returned us to the subject. "I bring up the matter of fighting in space for a reason. We intend to take the battle back to the Freds. We know that you and PFC Sanders"—he nodded in Arlene's direction—"have a unique capacity in this regard."

I knew that vacation time was over. I also wondered who the hell the Freds were.

Williams let us have it right between the ears. "Over a year ago, before I joined the team, this installation received a coherent signal from space. No other radio telescope picked it up. At first the men who received it thought it was mechanical failure or someone playing a joke on them. It could have come from a small radio a couple of klicks away, but it didn't."

He took a moment to check the notes on his clipboard. We all listened in rapt attention. I was ready to learn something new about the enemy, anything to speed up their final defeat.

"They analyzed the signal," he continued, "and established that it was a narrow-beam microwave transmission. There were variations and holes in the message. We did a sophisticated computer analysis using the Dornburg system, the best satellite-and-astronomy program ever developed. We were receiving a complex billiard-shot message that had been successively bounced off seven bodies in our solar system on its way to Earth. When we connected the various holes and occlusions, the result was an arrow leading straight out of the solar system, a line that could not have been faked. The message had to have originated outside the orbit of Pluto-Charon."

The director smiled. "Sorry if that was a bit technical, but it reminds me of what Robert Anton Wilson said: that if we find planets beyond Pluto, they should be named Mickey and Goofy. Charon is so small it's really only a moon of Pluto."

The admiral cleared his throat and stepped into the act: "There was an unexpected snag in the, er, handling of the data. The previous director decided not to tell the government about the message. The members of his team were divided in their sympathies as well."

Williams picked up the thread. "They were afraid the military-industrial complex would turn the whole thing into a big national security problem."

Arlene was standing right next to me and whispered

in my ear: "That sounds almost as bad as the Hollywood industrial complex."

"Hush," I hushed her.

The director continued. "The scientists spent months decoding the signal, but they made slow progress. Then they ran into a little interruption: the invasion came."

"Duh!" said Jill in my other ear, so I hushed her, too.

Williams didn't hear their sarcastic remarks, and the brass seemed to have been struck with temporary deafness, which was fine with me. I hoped there would be Q&A. I wanted to ask about the Freds.

Williams wasn't deaf, though. He reminded me of the nuns when they caught us whispering during a lesson. He frowned in our direction and became very serious. "In the wake of the invasion, my predecessor committed suicide. He blamed himself for not having passed the information on to Washington. In his defense, we might remember how certain agencies of the government turned traitor and collaborated with the Freds. Imagine selling out your own species to things you've never seen, about which you know less than nothing."

So that was it. The Freds were what they called the alien overlords behind our demonic playmates. I wondered how that name got started.

"I will never forget the traitors," Albert spoke from depths of a personal suffering I hope never to experience. The director didn't mind this interruption. He smiled and thanked Albert for his contribution.

That was all the invitation Arlene needed to get into the act. "Did we ever break the code?" she asked.

"That happened after Director Williams took over," the admiral volunteered.

"Many members of the original team are still here," the director quickly added. "They weren't held responsible for my predecessor's decision."

"We no longer enjoy the luxury of wasting our best brains," Kimmel added.

"We broke the code," said the director, returning to essentials. "The message was not what we expected. The alien message was a warning."

"A warning?" Arlene echoed him. "You mean a threat, an ultimatum?"

"No," Williams continued softly. "The aliens who sent the message were attempting to warn us about the impending invasion. You understand, don't you? There are *friendly* aliens out there, enemies of the Freds who warned us about these monsters who've invaded Earth. There's more."

I could tell that he was enjoying this, but I couldn't criticize him for his scientific joy. Part of his pleasure came from the discovery of an attempt to help the human race in its hour of need. But if he didn't get to the point real soon, I was prepared to change my evaluation of his character . . . sooner.

He continued: "These friendly aliens seem to be saying they are the ones who built the Gates on Phobos; but we're not certain of that. We are certain that they are inviting us to use these Gates to teleport to their base. We have the access codes. We even have the phone number. I mean to say they've sent us the teleportation coordinates. So the next step is obvious. We think it would be a good idea if certain experienced space marines delivered a return message—in person."

At first I was afraid they'd leave me behind. I'm a marine, but I've never been off-planet before. Of course, that shouldn't keep them from using me. No one else in the solar system has the experience of Fly and Arlene. They need two more people on the mission. I might as well be one of them.

Arlene and I have agreed not to mention my marriage proposal to the brass. We don't intend to keep it a secret from Fly or Jill, though. There'd really be no point to that. But I feel there was little point to my proposal in the first place. I'm honored that she is wearing my ring with her dog tags. I just hope it doesn't end up hanging from her toe along with the tag that goes there when a marine dies . . . and there's enough of a body left for identification.

I never dreamed I'd go into space. Now they're talking about our leaving the solar system. I don't know what to think. The brass, in their usual sensitive way, told me there's nothing to hold me on Earth except the law of gravity.

Right after Director Williams dropped his bombshell about the friendly aliens—and I'll believe it when I see them—the brass told Jill and me they had something important and personal to discuss with us. Fly and Arlene were still reeling from the bombshell, and the colonel wanted to see them privately.

So the director turned us over to a woman aptly named Griffin, who took us to a little room where she proceeded to give us a pop quiz. "Do you understand seismographic readings?" she asked.

"They show earthquakes," Jill piped up. "Do you understand decimal points?" she threw back at the woman in her most sarcastic voice.

The woman named Griffin had a stone face worthy of a Gorgon. She turned on a computer screen and started bringing up charts and numbers. "I won't bore you with the numbers," she said wearily. "Seismographic labs in Nevada and New Mexico detected five jolts that could only have been the result of a nuclear bombardment. The probable ground zero is Salt Lake City."

Jill and I looked at each other and saw our emotions reflected in each other's faces. Jill tried so hard not to cry that I couldn't stand it. I cried first, for both of us.

I thought about all those old comrades—Jerry, Nate, even the president of the Council of Twelve. They couldn't all be gone! I remembered two sisters who seemed to have been touched by the hand of God: Brinke and Linnea. I had helped them with their study of the Book of Mormon. They couldn't be gone, could they?

I hadn't admitted it to myself but until now an ultimate vindication of my faith was my certainty that Salt Lake City had been spared. That seemed to be incontrovertible evidence of the hand of God at work. We were, after all, the Church of the Latter-Day Saints. The whole point was our belief that the time of God's direct intervention was not over. His hand must still touch the world, else how could we be preserved after such a holocaust?

The Book of Mormon was still only a book, like the Bible or the Koran or the Talmud. Surviving in a world of real demons provided a sense of the supernatural that could barely be approached by every word of the First and Second Books of Nephi, Jacob, Enos, Jarom, Omni, the Words of Mormon, Book of Mosiah, Alma, Helaman, Third and Fourth Nephi, Book of Mormon, Esther, and Moroni. The scientific explanations carried only so much weight with me. That we could witness today's events made every holy text in the history of the human race seem more relevant to modern man.

If the Tabernacle had just been nuked, however, I needed to seriously rethink the prophecies.

Arlene looked fit and trim and beautifully deadly as we went to Colonel Hooker's office. This was no time for ladies first. I outranked her. I enjoyed outranking a woman who was fit and trim and beautifully deadly.

The door was already open, and the colonel was sitting behind his desk when I reached his threshold. It had been a long time since I'd pounded the pines. I stood in the doorway, raised my hand, and rapped on the doorframe three times, good and hard.

Colonel Hooker looked up with a grim expression. God only knew how many of us were left in the world. The best thing about being a marine is the pride, which gets back to the question of how a rabid individualist chooses to serve. When you're a marine, you *choose;* and men you respect must *choose* you, and respect is a two-way street paved with honor. Pity the poor monsters who got in our way.

"As you were," declared Hooker.

"Thank you, sir!" Arlene and I responded in unison.

We went into his office, and he offered us each one of his Afuente Gran Reserva cigars. They were big suckers. Too bad neither Arlene nor I smoked. He lit up and ordered us to become comfortable.

"I want to be certain you both understand the full implications," he said. "This is a four-man mission. The director has already pointed out your unique qualifications. We might as well be frank about it. This is not a mission from which anyone is expected to return."

I glanced over at Arlene without being too obvious about it. Her face was an impassive mask. She looks that way only when she is exerting superhuman control. It didn't take a telepath to read her thoughts: *Albert, Albert, Albert.*

The colonel must have had a telepathic streak himself. The next word out of his mouth was "Albert." Arlene's mask cracked to the extent that her eyes grew very wide. "Albert is my third choice for this mission," Hooker went on. "I've chosen him because of his record before the invasion and also because he's a veteran of fighting these damned monsters. Frankly, I don't think there are three other human beings alive who have had experiences to match yours."

"Probably not, sir," I agreed.

"If I were superstitious," he went on, "I'd say you lead charmed lives. We've come up with a mission to test that hypothesis. It will take a bit of doing, but you will have a ship and a navy crew to fly it."

"You said the marine operation is a four-man mission," Arlene reminded our CO. I loved the fact that she didn't say "four-person"—she never worries about that kind of junk.

"You'll be joined by another marine, a combat veteran," Hooker told us. I was glad to hear that. "Only marines go on this one. But we couldn't find anyone else with your particular background. Before you get acquainted with the new man, I have a present for you."

He reached into a desk drawer and took out two white envelopes with our names on them. My turn to be telepathic. The little voice in the back of my head hadn't worried about this kind of stuff for a long time. We'd been kind of busy staying alive and saving the universe.

But as I opened that envelope and saw the three chevrons of a sergeant, I felt a kind of quiet pride I'd almost forgotten. Those thin yellow stripes carried more meaning than I could have crammed into a dictionary. Arlene held her promotion out for me to see, trophies of war. A PFC no more, she had a stripe now: she was a lance corporal. Both the promotions carried the crossed swords design of the space marines.

Man, I felt great.

11

I didn't feel so great when I met the fourth member of our team. He was an officer! After all the big buildup about our unique status as space marines, they go and saddle us with a freakin' officer whose experience couldn't compare to ours, by their own admission. After mentally reviewing every joke I'd ever heard about military intelligence, I cooled off. Some wise old combat vet once said not all officers are pukeheads. Funny, I can't remember the wise old vet's name.

Captain Esteban Hidalgo did bring some assets to the mission. He was a good marine, with high honors from the New Mexico war. That was on the good side. Plenty of combat experience, but mainly against humans.

On the debit side, there was everything else. In five minutes I had him down in my book as a real martinet butthead. Admittedly, five minutes does not pass muster as a scientific sampling, but Hidalgo didn't help matters by the way he started off.

"One thing you both need to know about me up front," he barked out. "I don't fraternize. I insist upon military discipline and grooming. I demand that uniforms be kept polished and in good repair."

I couldn't believe what I was hearing. It was as if the past year had just evaporated. Never mind that the human race was facing the possibility of extinction. We had rules to follow. Throughout history there have been examples of this crap. If an outnumbered army starts to have success, it is essential that the high command assigns a by-the-book officer to remind the blooded combat veterans that victory is only a secondary goal. Respect for the command structure is what's sacred.

I could feel Hooker's eyes on me, watching every muscle quiver. Maybe the whole thing was a test. Fighting hell-princes was a walk in the park, obviously. Defeating the ultimate enemy could go to a fellow's head and make him forget the important things in life, like keeping his shoes spit-polished. I could just imagine us in the kind of nonstop jeopardy Arlene and I had barely lived through on Phobos and Deimos while Captain Hidalgo worried about the buttons on our uniforms.

"I've studied your combat records," he said. "Exemplary. Both of you. A word for you, Sergeant

Taggart. On Phobos and Deimos, you almost made up for your insubordination in Kefiristan."

Why was Hooker doing this? I wanted to rip off Hidalgo's neat Errol Flynn mustache and shove it down his throat. But I took a page from Arlene's book and arranged my face into an impassive mask equal to anything in a museum. Hooker scrutinized me throughout this ordeal. So did Arlene.

Finally hell in Hawaii ended, and we were dismissed. We had a lot to do before the final briefing. We had to go rustle up Albert and Jill. Turned out she could be part of the first phase of our new mission, if she wanted to be. She was a civilian and a kid, though, so no one was going to order her. And I was certain we would all want to say our good-byes to Ken. Mulligan, too.

I insisted that Arlene and I take the long way around to finding our buds. It may only be residual paranoia from my school days, but I felt better about discussing the teacher outdoors. They don't bug the palm trees this side of James Bond movies.

"So how do you feel about our promotions?" Arlene asked.

"Every silver lining has a cloud," I replied.

"I could feel how tense you were in there about our new boss."

"You weren't exactly mellow about Albert."

"Mixed feelings, Fly. I'm weighing never seeing him again against his joining us on another suicide mission."

"If Hidalgo has anything to say about it—"

"Let's talk, Fly. I know you as well as I know myself, and I think you're overreacting. Just because the man is a stickler for the rules doesn't make him another Lieutenant Weems. Remember, Weems broke the rules when he ordered his men to open fire on the monks."

She had a point there. Arlene had been on my side from the start of the endlessly postponed court-martial of Corporal Flynn Taggart.

My turn: "There's nothing we can do if this officer is a butthead." I'd never liked officers, but I followed orders. It annoyed me a little that Arlene got along so well with officers.

"I'll tell you exactly what we're going to do," she said, and I could tell she'd given the problem considerable thought. "You are too concerned over the details, Fly. I don't care if Hidalgo wants my uniform crisp so long as it's possible to accommodate such a request without endangering the mission. All I care about is that the captain knows what he's doing."

"Fair enough, but I'll need a lot of convincing."

Arlene chuckled softly. "You know, Fly, there are some people who would think we're bad marines. Some people only approve of the regulation types."

"We saw how well those types did on Phobos."

"Exactly."

"Now we're going back. So stop holding out on me. You were gonna say something about Captain Hidalgo."

She frowned. "Simple. While he's deciding if we measure up to his standards, we'll be deciding if he measures up to ours. This is the most serious war in the history of the human race. The survival of the species is at stake. My first oath of allegiance is to homo sapiens. That comes before loyalty to the corps. We can't afford to make any mistakes. We won't."

I got her general drift, but I couldn't believe what I

was hearing. "What if Hidalgo doesn't measure up to our standards?"

We'd been walking slowly around the perimeter of the building. She stopped and eyeballed me. "First we must reach the Gates on Phobos. We weren't the greatest space pilots when we brought that shoebox from Deimos to Earth. You may be the finest jet pilot breathing, but we can learn a few things about being space cadets. We're just extra baggage until we're back on our own turf. That's when we'll really become acquainted with Captain Hidalgo."

"God, who would've thought there'd come a day when we'd think of that hell moon as our turf!"

She gave me her patented raised-eyebrow look. "Fly, we're the only veterans of the Phobos-Deimos War. And the only experts."

She was keeping something from me. I wasn't going to let this conversation terminate until she fessed up. "Agreed. So what do we do about Hidalgo if he doesn't measure up?"

"Simple," she said. "We'll space his ass right out the airlock."

"You don't have to go to Phobos, Jill."

I appreciated Ken telling me that. "I want to go. Arlene and Fly wouldn't know what to do without me. Besides, they couldn't have saved me without you."

"That's true," said Fly.

Ken was sitting up in bed. He'd wanted to see us off from his wheelchair, but he'd been working hard and had tired himself. His face was a healthy coffee color again. When he was first unwrapped, his skin had been pale and sickly. They unwrapped him in stages so for a while he had stripes like a zebra as his color returned. Now he looked like himself again, except for the knobs and wire things that they hadn't taken out of his head yet.

"I'm grateful to all of you," he said. "Especially you, Jill," he added, taking my hand. "But you're so young. You've been in so much danger already. Why not stay here where it's safe?"

"Safe?" echoed Albert.

"I should say safer," said Ken.

Arlene brought up a subject that Albert and I had avoided: "Before we left Salt Lake City, there were people who thought it would be better for Jill to stay there."

Ken coughed. He sounded really bad. I brought him a glass of water. "I feel so helpless," he said. "You only need Jill's computer assistance on the first leg of the mission. If only there were some way I could help by long-distance."

"You've put your finger on the problem," Fly told him. "We can't anticipate everything we're going to need. Too bad Jill is the best troubleshooter for this job."

"Just like before," I reminded everyone. "You should take me to space with you, too."

"That's not part of the deal," said Arlene, sounding like a mother.

"We should be grateful for this time together," Albert pointed out. He was right. The only people with Ken were Fly, Arlene, Albert, and me. The mission would start tomorrow morning.

"If only they had launch capability in the islands here," Ken complained. "They should have been better prepared."

"We're fortunate they have as much as they do,"

argued Arlene. "There's everything here except the kitchen sink."

"The kitchen sink is what we need, and it's at Point Mugu," said Fly. "Thanks to Ken, we have a launch window."

"I never thought I'd do windows," Ken rasped between fits of coughing. "I always say that when you take off for a body in space it's a good idea for your destination to be there when you arrive! It's also nice to have a crew to fly the ship. The primary plan to return Fly and Arlene to Phobos has all the elegance of a Rube Goldberg contraption."

"I don't even feel homesick," said Arlene. Everyone laughed.

Ken had paid us back big time for saving him from the spider-mind. He was smarter than I was about lots of things. I also realized he cared about me; but I don't think he realized how much I wanted to go with the others.

"There's a fallback plan?" Albert asked.

Ken smiled. "The less said about that the better, at least by me. Before you depart, I want to talk to Jill some more. I have some suggestions for her return trip."

"I want to go to Phobos," I said.

Every time I said that, Arlene repeated the same word: "No."

Fly sounded like a father when he said, "Believe me, if there were any other way, I'd never dream of taking Jill back into danger . . . well, greater danger, anyhow. We do need her for this."

"We're all needed," said Ken in a sad voice. "We'll all be needed for the rest of our lives, however short they may be." He looked at me again. "But I agree with you about one thing."

"What?"

"It's important to fight to the end. Sometimes I forget that."

"After what you've been through—" Arlene began, but he wouldn't let her finish.

"No excuses," he said. "I've been too ready to give up. But then I think about the terrible things these monsters have done to us, and it makes me angry. We will fight. So long as there are Jills, the human race has a chance."

I saw a tear in his eye. I was going to say something, but I suddenly couldn't remember what. Instead I went over to Ken and hugged him. He held me and kissed me on the forehead.

"You know, as long as we're all together again, there's a question I've been meaning to ask," Fly threw out.

"Shoot," said Albert.

"Bad choice of words around marines," said Ken.

"Civilians," said Arlene. She made it sound like a bad word.

Fly asked his question: "I keep meaning to ask one of the old hands around here: why are the masterminds behind the monsters called Freds?"

"I know, I know," I piped up. "I heard that sergeant gun guy talking about it."

"Master gun, hon," Arlene corrected. When she didn't sound like a mom she sure came off like a teacher.

I finished up: "Anyway, that man said a marine named Armogida started calling them Freds after he took a date to a horror movie."

"I wonder what movie it was," wondered Arlene.

"Well, maybe we should start calling our heroic young people Jills," Ken brought the subject back to me. "I can't change anyone's mind, so let me say I hope your mission goes well."

As I said, I appreciated Ken worrying about me. He just didn't understand how important it was to me that I go along. Fly promised I'd get to ride a surfboard.

12

The last thing I needed was a brand-new monster, fresh off the assembly line. For this, Fly, Albert, Jill, Captain Hidalgo, and I had traveled all the way to the mainland? For this, we'd taken a voyage in a cramped submarine meant for half the number of personnel aboard? (Of course, the sub seemed like spacious accommodations after the shuttle we'd built on Deimos.) I mean, I was all set to encounter new cosmic horrors when we returned to the great black yonder. Arlene, astrogator and monster-slayer—I'm available for the job at reasonable rates! But none of us were prepared for what awaited us in the shallows off good old California.

The military airfield at Point Mugu is about five miles south of Oxnard. When we passed the Channel Islands, Captain Ellison told us we'd be offshore—as close to land as the sub dared—in about thirty minutes. Of course he used naval time. After spending years in uniform, I'm surprised I prefer thinking in civilian terms for time, distances, and holidays.

The trip had been uneventful, except for Jill hassling me about what a great asset she would be to the mission if we took her to Phobos. I finally got tired of her and suggested she bug Captain Hidalgo. After all, he was in charge. Too much of Jill and I thought our marine officer might be willing to space himself.

Hidalgo handled Jill very well. He simply told her that her part of the mission would be finished at the base. He also reminded her that Ken had gone to a lot of trouble to work out a plan for her return trip, and she didn't want to let him down, did she? Then he wouldn't listen to her anymore. In some respects Hidalgo was more qualified to be a father than Fly was. But that didn't prove that he had what it took to save the universe from galactic meanies. That was sort of a specialized field.

I'd never been aboard a submarine before. I disliked the odor. In working hard to eliminate the men's-locker-room aroma, they had come up with something a lot worse, something indescribable—at least by me.

The captain of the sub was a good officer. Ellison was plenty tough and well qualified for the job. He was almost apologetic when he explained how we were expected to go ashore.

"You're kidding," said Albert.

"Surfboards," repeated Captain Ellison. "We have four long boards for the adults and a boogie board for the . . ." He saw Jill glaring at him and choked off the word he was about to say. "The smaller board is for Jill. It was especially designed for her body size."

"Neat," said Jill, mollified. "It's just like Fly promised."

"Why are we going in by surfboard?" I heard myself ask.

Fly shrugged. He'd found out about it before Jill or I had. That didn't mean he approved.

Hidalgo had a ready answer. "So the enemy won't find a raft or other evidence of a commando raid."

I should have kept my mouth shut. I was the one telling Fly to hold off on passing judgment. But I didn't seem able to keep certain words from coming out: "You think these demons can make fine distinctions like that, the same as a human enemy in a human war?"

Captain Hidalgo believed in dealing with insubordination right away. "First, this is a decision from above, Lance Corporal. We will follow orders. Second, there are human traitors, in case you don't remember. They might be able to make these distinctions. Third, we will not take any unnecessary chances. Fourth, I refer you to my first point. Got it?"

"Yes, sir." I said it with sincerity. He did have a point, or two.

When Jill got me alone—not an easy thing to do on a sub—she said, "Hooray. We get to surf!"

"Have you ever ridden a board?" I asked.

"Well, no," she admitted, "but I've been to the beach plenty of times and seen how it's done."

Oh, great, I thought.

"Have you?" she asked.

"As a matter of fact, I have. We've just left the ideal place to learn. Hawaii. They have real waves there. You can get a large enough wave to shoot the curl."

"Huh?"

91

This was looking less and less promising. I explained: "The really large waves create a semi-tunnel that you can sort of skim through. You've seen it in movies."

"Oh, sure. But we won't have waves that large off L.A., will we?"

She was a smart kid. "No, we shouldn't. We'll be dropped near a beach north of L.A. This time of the year, with no storms, the waves should be gentle."

Jill wasn't through with me. "How hard can it be to hang on to our boards and just let the waves take us in?"

She had me there. It wasn't as if we needed to show perfect form and win prizes. We simply had to make it to the beach. The equipment and provisions were in watertight compartments. They'd float better than we would. Each of us would be responsible for specific items, and they'd be attached to us. All in all, getting to shore should be a relatively simple matter.

Only trouble was that none of us had counted on the appearance of a brand-new monster.

Actually, there had been intimations of this new critter on the last day Fly and I had spent on the beach at Oahu. When the admiral noticed the lone cloud drifting in, there was no reason to doubt that we were looking at a cloud. Later, when Fly and I noticed the black triangle cutting through the water, we naturally assumed it was a shark. We didn't pay any attention to the sky. If we had, we would have noticed that the cloud had disappeared. We might have wondered about that.

When the sub surfaced as close to shore as Ellison was willing to go, the Big Four gathered for our last adventure. It was a strange feeling that Jill was not going all the way. Hidalgo would replace her when we reached the spacecraft.

I didn't want Jill to accompany us on a journey that might be a suicide mission. On the other hand, I didn't like the idea of leaving her behind in California doom. Hidalgo had assured Big Daddy Fly and me that the plan for Jill's return to Hawaii was foolproof. Ken would never have said that, though the plan was his. Guarantees like that are offered by fools.

The plan, however, hadn't taken into account the fluffy white cloud descending toward the water as we paddled around on our fiberglass boards. We were outfitted in our wet suits, floundering around in the calm area, waiting for some wave action. Fly was first to notice the cloud coming right down to the surface and then sort of seeping into the water. Not vanishing. Not evaporating. "Seeping" was the only way to describe the cloud as its color changed to a vague green and it sort of flowed into the water.

"What the hell was that?" asked Fly.

"It's right in front of us," observed Hidalgo.

"That's unnatural," shouted the sub's captain from the conning tower. He was too decent a man to submerge again until he knew we were all right.

"Maybe it's weird weather," suggested Jill quite reasonably.

I could believe that. So much radiation and crap had been bombarding Mother Earth that she might have some surprises of her own. But after fighting the alien denizens of hell, I was suspicious of anything unusual. When I saw a shark fin appear right where the cloud had joined with the ocean, I became a lot more suspicious.

By then Hidalgo and Albert had caught the first

wave. They were on their bellies, on their boards, paddling with their hands. I'd told everyone to go all the way in to shore without standing up. The boards would keep even a natural landlubber afloat.

The rest of us caught the next gentle swell that would take us toward the beach. That was when I saw three fins circling the spot where the cloud had gone into the water.

Naturally, I thought they were sharks. That was adequate cause to worry. The fin of a surfboard and its white underbelly looks like a fish. The paddling hands and kicking feet attract attention, too. It wasn't as if our team was made up of people who could surf their way out of danger; and the waves weren't providing anything to write about.

"Shark!" I shouted. The others started repeating the call. We would have continued thinking the fins belonged to separate creatures if they didn't start rising out of the water. What appeared to be long black ropes writhed up out of the sea. Hidalgo and Albert paddled furiously to change direction, but the current continued drawing them toward the thing.

As the huge creature continued to rise, I expected to make out more details. But it seemed to bring a fog with it. The mantle surrounding the thing was the same white as the cloud.

Within the mist, I could see fragments of recognizable objects. A slight breeze was blowing in toward the shore, but the fog didn't dissipate. The stuff hung on like sticky cotton; but gaps did open up where I could see more.

A claw. An eye. A large glistening red opening in a larger dark surface that seemed to open and close. Could this be a mouth? None of us needed to know that answer all that badly. The entity constantly shifted. I got a headache from trying to focus on it. One moment the black surface seemed to have a metallic sheen. The next moment the surface rippled as only a living thing could do. All through my attempt to see what we were fighting, the mist remained a problem, changing in density but never going away.

Most of our weapons were secured in the waterproof packages, but Fly had put a gun in a plastic bag and zipped it inside his suit. He got it out with admirable speed and started firing at the whatsit. He'd picked out a nice little customized Ruger pistol for this part of the mission. He could be like a kid in the candy store when let loose in a decent armory; and Hawaii currently had a lot more in its arsenal than ornate war clubs.

He felt better after he'd fired off a few rounds. I felt better, too. Near as I could tell, the horrible inexplicable thing from the sky felt absolutely nothing. Fly demonstrated his skill, again, for what it was worth. Although he was behind Albert and Hidalgo, his bullets came nowhere near hitting them. Every shot went right into the center of the roiling mass—and probably out the other side if the monster had the power to discorporate, which I was ready to believe. Fly got off all his shots while lying on his belly and hanging on to his board. He really is very good at what he does.

Suddenly someone got off a shot that made a difference. A sound of thunder from behind, a whistling-screaming over our heads, and an explosion that knocked all of us off our boards.

Ellison had the largest gun and he wasn't afraid to

use it. The shell struck the creature at dead center. I wasn't sure this monster could be killed, but the submarine captain's quick thinking made the new menace go away.

Jill literally whooped for joy. She waved back at the submarine, but I doubt they saw her. I barely saw her. We were surrounded by mist from the explosion. So much water turned into steam that I wondered if the shell had set off something combustible in the monster. Maybe we were receiving residue from the sticky cloud-fog stuff. One thing was certain: we wouldn't be doing any scientific analysis out here.

Hidalgo performed his duty: "Everyone sing out! Let me hear you."

"Sanders!" I shouted back at him.

"Taggart!"

"Gallatin!"

"I'm here," Jill finished the roster.

"Name!" Hidalgo insisted, and then took a moment to cough up some water.

"I'm Jill. Sheesh."

"Last name!" Hidalgo insisted.

"Lovelace," she finally relented.

Meanwhile, the sun was climbing in the morning sky. I was getting hot inside my wet suit. The sub was now far enough behind us that it counted as history. Before us was the future, where the breaking surf became white spray to cover the white droppings of seagulls. I'd never been so happy to see those scavenger birds. Some things on the home planet were still normal.

13

"**W**hat do you mean you hate zero-g?" Arlene asked with genuine surprise.

"Just do," I said.

"You never told me that."

"You never asked."

Arlene was not an easy person to surprise. I wasn't sure why the subject had never come up. I wasn't deliberately holding out on her. Jill laughed—the little eavesdropper.

"You never cease to amaze me, Fly Taggart," Arlene continued. "Here we've traveled half the solar system together."

"Now, that's an exaggeration," I pointed out, unwilling to let her get away with—

"Hyperbole," she explained, showing that she'd been an English major once upon a time.

"Yeah, right," I said. "We've only done the hop from Earth to Mars and back again."

"Some hop," Albert replied good-naturedly.

"Please, Albert." Arlene put her foot down. "This is a private conversation."

"Private?" Jill echoed. "Inside here?"

"Here" was the cockpit of a DCX-2004. It had been christened the *Bova*. From the outside, it looked like a nose cone that someone had stretched and then added fins along the bottom. But when you got closer and saw it outlined against the night sky, you realized it was a big mother of a ship. Even so, it was cramped for four of us in a space designed only for the pilot and copilot. Hidalgo was outside the craft, taking the first watch. He'd warn us if a certain large hell-prince woke up. He would also let us know if anyone showed up who could fly this baby.

Plan A had worked fine so far. We were all alive. We were in the right place. So what if the others—people we'd never seen—were late? So what that they were supposed to be here ahead of us? Plan A still beat the hell out of plan B.

We figured it was only right to let Jill see the inside of her first spaceship. She hadn't stopped hinting she wanted to come along. We weren't going to lie to her about having calculated the weight of our crew to the last ounce. The ship's mass factor could accommodate Jill. There was even room if we didn't mind being very crowded instead of only really crowded. (Elbow room was already out of the question.)

Of course, all this would be academic if we didn't get our navy crew. None of us could fly this tub. Whether the crew showed up or not didn't change one fact: Jill wasn't invited on the trip. It was as simple as that.

One advantage to showing her the interior of the ship was that she could see for herself that there was absolutely nowhere for a stowaway to hide. At times like this I was grateful the bad guys hadn't figured out how to manufacture itty-bitty demons. The pumpkins were as small as they got. So if a guy was in close quarters he didn't have to worry about Tinker Bell with mini-rockets. Life was good.

The *Bova* was a lot bigger than the submarine. That didn't mean we had any space to waste inside. Looked to me as if the primary function of the ship was to transport tanks and fuel. Human beings would be allowed to tag along if they didn't get in the way.

Anyway, Albert had a ready answer to Jill's challenge about the lack of privacy: "When the CO is away," he told her, "the men can shoot the shit." I never thought I'd hear Albert talk like that, but then I realized what a decent thing he'd done.

This could be the last time any of us saw Jill. Albert was treating her like one of the men. She knew how religious he was. For him to use that kind of language in front of her meant something special. Jill smiled at Albert. He returned the smile. They'd connected.

"Look, Arlene," I said, attempting to wrap up our pointless conversation. "When they advertise the honeymoon suites in free fall, I'm not the target audience. I wouldn't try to make love in one of those for free. On Phobos, whenever I went outside the artificial gravity area, I had a tougher time from that than anything the imps did to me. If the ones I encountered in zero-g had known about my weakness, it would have been another weapon on their side. Hey, I don't like bleeding to death, either. That doesn't stop me from fighting the bastards."

"No, Fly, it doesn't," said Arlene, touching my arm. I noticed Albert noticing. He wasn't very obvious about it. I don't think it was any kind of jealousy when Arlene was physical with another person. Albert's affection for her was so great that he couldn't help being protective.

"I never mentioned the weightless thing before," I

went on, more bugged than I'd realized, "because I didn't want to give you cause for concern."

She switched from the tone of voice she used for kidding around to the steady, serious tone she used with a comrade. "I never would have known if you hadn't told me," she said. "You're a true warrior, Fly. Your hang-ups are none of my business unless you decide to make them my business."

We sat there in close quarters, sizing each other up as we had so many times before. She was quite a gal, Arlene Sanders.

"What's it like?" Jill asked.

"What?" I threw back, a little dense all of a sudden.

"Being weightless," Jill piped in. She thought we were still on that subject. Can't blame her for not realizing we'd moved on to grown-up stuff.

Arlene returned to teacher mode. "Well, it's like at the amusement parks when you ride a roller coaster and you go over the top, and you feel the dip in the pit of your stomach."

"Like on the parachute ride," Jill spoke from obvious experience. "Or when you fall. That's why it's called—what did Fly call it?"

"Free fall," I repeated.

"I don't mind that for a little bit," Jill admitted. "But how can you stand it for—"

"Weeks and weeks?" Arlene finished helpfully.

Jill bit her bottom lip, something she did only when she was thinking hard. Right now you could see the thought right on her face: Do I really want to go into space?

"You become used to it," Arlene told her.

"Yeah," said Jill, not really looking at us. Like most brilliant people, she thought out loud some of the time. She was staring at the bulkhead, probably imagining herself conquering the spaceways. "I can get used to anything."

Then she looked at each of us in turn. First Arlene, then Albert, then me. Finally the reality sank in. We were going to separate, probably forever.

"You can't leave me," she whispered, but all of us heard her.

"We don't have any choice," Albert replied almost as softly.

"But you told me people always have a choice," Jill wailed at the man she'd known longer than any other adult. "You're always talking about free will and stuff."

"I don't want to split up," said Albert. "I'm worried about you, but I know you can take care of yourself."

"I don't want to take care of myself," she almost screamed. The ship was soundproof, so she could make all the noise she wanted to without waking the demons. But as I saw her face grow red in anguish, I wished Arlene and I were still arguing about zero-g. Anything but this.

"You can't fool me," she said, addressing all of us. If looks could have killed, we would've been splattered over the acceleration couches like yesterday's pumpkins.

Then she let us have it with both barrels: "You don't love me!"

It's not fair. After everything we've done together, they want to get rid of me. I'm a problem to them. They won't admit it. They'll say they want to protect me. I'll bet everything in the world that's what they'll say next. It's for my own good, and they don't want me going into danger again. Blah, blah, blah, blah.

What can we run into in space that's any scarier than the sea monster that almost got us when we were surfing in to shore? What could be more dangerous than when I was almost crushed like a bug when I helped save Ken from the spider-mind and the steam demon on the train? Or when I was driving the truck and the two missiles from the bony almost got me? (Poor Dr. Ackerman called those things revenants. Boy, he sure came up with some weird names. He said all the creatures were like monsters from the id. I wonder what he meant.)

It's not just about danger. Everywhere is dangerous now. Who says I'll make it back to Hawaii alive? Even if everything goes according to plan, the return trip will take weeks. I might be safer going into space with them. But grown-ups don't want to have a kid around, 'specially not a teenager, so they lie, lie, lie.

They won't even admit how much they need me. After we reached shore, we didn't simply walk to the rocket field. I helped a lot. When it looked as if we might not get in, Arlene reminded everyone of Plan B. Ken was right. Plan B is a joke.

Plan B called for them to get on one of the alien rockets as stowaways. I threw a fit when I heard about that. They thought I was upset because they wouldn't let me come along. And they think I'm a dumb kid! I pointed out they could never stay hidden all the way to Mars on something as small as a rocket.

Phobos and Deimos are very small moons, but they are a lot larger than an alien rocket. Fly and Arlene hadn't even managed to stay hidden on the Martian moons. They'd told us about their adventures so many times I could recite the stories backwards. If they couldn't avoid the demons on Deimos and the former humans on Phobos, they wouldn't be able to stay hidden on a spaceship all the way to Mars—and Arlene has the nerve to tell me not to think about stowing away on this ship? She must think I'm really dense.

I wonder if they're mad because Captain Hidalgo agreed with me that stowing away on an alien ship was stupid. He prefers taking his chances on one of our own ships to "climbing into bed with the devil," even if we have to fly it ourselves. But then it was Fly's turn to point out that without the navy guys, we can't even try to take this ship up. He's done so many impossible things already that I guess he knows what a real impossibility looks like.

Maybe I'm better off without them. If they don't want me, they don't have to bother with me any longer. Getting here wasn't easy. Getting inside was even harder. Who was it that jammed computer systems and electronic devices? The person I saw reflected in a window sure looked a lot like me! We hardly ran into any monsters until we entered the base. (Maybe they were all on vacation.) The ones inside seemed to be asleep. I'd never seen them sleep before. I didn't know they slept at all. Poor Fly and Arlene were all set to shoot 'em up, but they didn't have any moving targets this time.

Poor Fly.

Poor Arlene.

I won't pick on Albert about this. He's not as much a nonstop marine as they are. But I didn't think Albert would ever leave me. Until now I was sure he'd figure out some way for them to take me along. How can he abandon me? We've been together since Salt Lake City. I guess none of us expected to be alive this long.

Now I'm supposed to go back to Hawaii. I always wanted to see Maui.

I wish they'd just tell me they don't like me anymore, or that they never liked me. I never wanted a family. I didn't mind being an orphan. But now I feel what it's like to have a family. We've had some of it. I don't want it to end.

I'm so angry I don't know what I want. They won't see me cry, though. I won't let them see me cry.

I knew it would come to this. It would be my job because I'm the woman, the adult woman. Fly became so much like a real father to Jill that he couldn't put his foot down. All he could do was spoil his darling little girl, the apple of his eye.

So I have the thrill of playing Mom. Jill was born difficult. It was completely against her nature to make this kind of situation easy.

"We are leaving you here," I told her, "because we do love you. It's time you have a reality check. You are not a child. You are not a little girl anymore. You have proved yourself to all of us. We know it. You know it. This is no time to start acting like a little girl."

"Then why—"

"Shut up!" I cut her off. This was no time to be diplomatic, either. "Don't say one word until I've finished. You were right about not trying to stow away on an alien ship when we have other options. But we wouldn't have let you join us in sneaking aboard an enemy craft, and we won't let you come with us now because we will be in combat sooner or later."

She stared at me with the kind of fixed concentration that meant only one thing. She was trying to hold back tears.

"You can do anything you want, Jill," I said, trying

my best to sound like a friend instead of Mommy. "You're a woman. You can marry, have babies, take up arms, join what's left of the real marines—the ones on our side—and fight the traitors. Society has been destroyed, Jill. You'll have a hand in shaping the new society. You're staying behind on Earth. The rest of us may never see home again. You're probably more important to the future of mankind than we are. But hear this: you cannot come with us! Do you understand?"

She looked me in the eye for several seconds. I thought she wanted to kill me. Then she said very slowly, "I understand."

I believed her.

14

I can see clearly in the moonlight, and I wish for darkness. If I can see them, they can see me. As I stare into the face of the minotaur, I remember how my wife died: one of these things killed her. Our families were so sympathetic. We had a big funeral. The neighborhood we lived in wasn't a war zone yet. She'd been caught outside in no-man's-land. For her, it was no-Mrs.-Hidalgo-land.

We hadn't told our families we were getting a

divorce. We both came from strong Catholic families. So we put off telling them, and then one of the demons made our wedding vows come true—the part about till death do us part. She hated me at the end, with the kind of hatred that comes only from spoiled love. It became so bad I couldn't even look at her anymore.

I was standing outside the DCX-2004, waiting for our navy space crew, so this seemed like a good time to be honest with myself. Colonel Hooker didn't know what went on between my wife and me. I never told him I was suicidal for a while. It wasn't something I was proud of: I was suicidal before the minotaur slaughtered her; I wasn't suicidal afterward.

Everyone was at the funeral, assuming a grief I didn't feel; all of them assumed I'd devote the rest of my life to avenging the woman I loved. A marine is supposed to be at home in a world of hurt. There's no personal problem that can't be solved by picking up an M92 and doing your part for Uncle Sam. Right. *Sí.*

But my military operational specialty was killing an enemy that could shoot back. I wasn't prepared to find out that my wife had aborted our child. Until that moment, I had no idea how much she detested being married to a marine. She said my loyalty to the Corps came before my love for her and I'd treat our son the same way I'd treated her.

I didn't know I had a son until after the abortion. Then I looked at her with a hatred I'd never felt for any human enemy, and a hatred I've yet to feel for these devils from space. At that moment I felt like apologizing to all the opponents I'd ever wasted.

I thought about killing her. I even started to formulate a plan. Then the monsters came, and our personal problems went on the back burner for a while. I was off fighting the war to begin all wars, and she was safe at home, just waiting for a big red minotaur to turn her into a taco with special sauce.

The timing on all this was interesting. If she'd had the abortion after the invasion and said she couldn't bear to bring up our child in a hell on Earth, I would have been pissed but I might have been able to forgive her. No, the timing was lousy . . . for her. I was called up right away, so I wasn't around for her to realize how much I'd turned against her.

I was only a little suicidal on the mission against the arachnotrons. Leave it to the military to come up with a name like that. We called them spider-babies. We called ourselves the Orkin squad. We did a fine job of exterminating them.

When I returned home and finally had it out with my wife, the marital battlefield seemed like a restful picnic, She gave me a bunch of feminist crap. I told her she was a spoiled brat who obviously hadn't been punished enough when she was growing up. I was mad. She didn't like my attitude.

Then I saw a side of her that completely surprised me. After you've been married to someone for years, you'd think you'd pick up on the important aspects of that person's character. I'd never had a clue that she felt the way she did until she accused me of always sucking up to the Anglos! She insisted that I was a bad Latino. In her mind, I suppose that made her a wonderful Latina.

I'd never thought about my ethnic identity all that much, even when I was growing up. I tried not to pay attention to it. Sometimes it struck me funny the way the American media always presented the problems of the cities as black versus white, as though all the colors in between didn't matter. Now we have new colors to worry us—the bright colors of the scales and leathery hides of the invaders. The devils.

Of course I had experienced my fair share of prejudice. I first came to America as an illegal immigrant. I wasn't here for the welfare, but I wasn't willing to wait in line forever. I came to America for the dream. I came to work and go to college.

I met a young lawyer who was sympathetic to what I was trying to do. Pat Hoin was her name, my first Anglo friend. She encouraged me to take advantage of one of the periodic amnesties when illegals could become legal. I did just that.

She thought I might have a bit too much pride for my own good. There was truth in that. Although I'd grown up in Mexico, I came from a very proud Spanish family. My father was so intent that I marry "someone worthy" that he helped drive me away from home. How ironic the way things turned out. He finally accepted my wife. Then she turned out to be treacherous.

The last time I saw Rita, we argued about anything and everything. Nothing was too trivial. After she exhausted the subject of my emotional failings, there remained the cosmic threat of my snoring. She failed to convince me that my snoring was on a scale with an army of zombies shuffling through the old community cemetery.

Somehow I had a last shred of feeling for her. When I reached out to touch her for the last time, she screamed that I was never to touch her again without permission.

I stormed out of there, leaving the next move to her. Here was the world coming to an end, and we couldn't take a break from our own stupid soap opera. So when I saw her face in the open coffin—they'd recovered only the top third of her body, but that was the important part for any good mortician—I looked down at her with such a grim expression that her sister, misinterpreting my solemnity, took me by the arm and whispered, "You'll get over it. You'll find someone else like her."

Only marine training prevented me from laughing out loud. As was the custom of our families, we took turns kissing her cold lips. It was the first time I'd enjoyed kissing her in a long time.

Now I'm supposed to be back on the job, working to save the human race. Well, why not? I don't suppose we're any worse than this big, bloated minotaur snoring in front of me. Let's see, now, Taggart and Sanders call it a hell-prince. The brain boys back at HQ call it a baron of hell.

I know a minotaur when I see one. Wait a minute. I've heard the others call it a minotaur, too. I know Jill did. She's quite a kid. A bit sullen and stuck-up but that's to be expected when you're fourteen. I kind of like her. She's strangely honest. She could grow up to be an honest woman. Anything is possible.

They have their chance to say their good-byes now. If the navy doesn't show, we'll probably never make it out of here alive. We'll try to stow away on one of the enemy ships, however slight our chance for survival. Our chances won't be good even if the navy space crew joins us, but at least the odds will be worth betting on.

If we make it to Phobos, then Taggart, Sanders, and Gallatin will become my headache. I wish I had a different team. Their combat records are fine. I'm not worried about that. I'm concerned about taking a triangle on the mission. Sanders and Gallatin want to screw each other's brains out. I'd have to be blind not to notice that. The mystery is where the hell Taggart fits in. I'm sure it's somewhere.

I don't need this crap on a mission. That's why I have to be a hard-ass. I'm going to keep them so busy that they won't have time to fool around. I'm not motivated by what happened to me with my wonderful, loving, faithful wife. I'm sure that's not it.

The mission is what concerns me . . . us! It has to. It's too damned important for lovesick marines to mess up. However slim the chances for success, I must guarantee maximum commitment.

Funny. Now that I'm thinking this way, the mission just got a boost in the arm. My grandmother believed in good omens. Up ahead, washed in moonlight, tiptoeing around our sleeping monster, it sure looks like the navy has arrived.

I'll never admit this to Fly but right at the end, I almost cried. Jill finally stopped arguing. She came over and hugged me. Then, without saying a word, she did the same to Fly and Albert. I was stunned. She stood in the open hatch, her back to us as if she couldn't decide if she wanted to do something.

She turned around and said, "I'll never forget any of you." Then she did the most amazing thing of all: Jill saluted us.

Of course none of us returned the salute. We're all conditioned marine robots. Mustn't ever break the precious rules. There are rules about who and when and what and where to exchange a precious salute. If Jill took seriously my offhand comment about joining the marines, she might earn the right to dress the way we do and perform the rituals. Maybe she'd wear a high-and-tight if she proved herself macho enough to earn the right, like me. Like me.

I didn't return her salute. But I made myself say, "Thank you, Jill. You are a true hero."

Then that spry little teenager walked out of my life. As she clocked out, the new cast of characters clocked in. Hidalgo came bounding up those same stairs like a kid who's gotten everything he wants for Christmas. For a moment, I didn't recognize him. It was the first time I'd seen him smile. He had the face of a man who believed in the mission. Absolutely.

He brought us a fine crew to pilot the barge. God knows how they arrived here. I hadn't seen any of them in Hawaii. When I asked where they'd been, I was rebuked with my least favorite word in the English language: "classified."

I didn't press the subject. I would have been happy to press their uniforms if that was what it took to keep everyone happy. They'd been outfitted with brand-new flight suits, combat boots, inflatable vests, helmets, gloves. . . . They looked a lot better than we did. I'd have liked to know how they did it.

Fly's big grin reminded me of arguments we used to have about luck. How he could live through what he had and not believe in good luck was beyond me. The moment we found all the demon guards asleep, I started believing in luck again. I'll take good omens where I can find them, too. Maybe the doom demons are becoming careless when we can penetrate a base so easily. That means we just might win the war.

The woman running the show inspired confidence: Commander Dianne Taylor. She was five feet four, weighing in at about one hundred pounds, with beautiful hazel eyes. I felt that we'd traded in a young female computer whiz for an older female space pilot. There was another woman on board as well, the petty officer, second class. For some time now, I hadn't been the only girl among the boys. I loved the fact that men with SEAL training had to answer to a female PO2.

"I'm a big enthusiast on the history of space flight," Commander Taylor addressed the latest member of the Big Four. "This ship is the latest generation of the old DC-X1 Delta Clipper. Basic principles remain the same."

"That's why we have faith in them," volunteered Albert.

"Exactly," replied our skipper happily. She was a natural teacher. That could take some of the boredom out of the trip. "The fuel is the same for the 2004 as for the first in the series—good old hydrogen peroxide."

I laughed. She raised an eyebrow in my general direction and I answered the unasked question. "I was thinking I could do my hair in it." She returned the laugh minus some interest: she allowed herself a smile.

"Or we can fuel up with hyper-vodka and have martinis with what's left over," she suggested. "Well, just as long as we all understand what the primary risk will be in taking off."

"What's that?" asked Hidalgo as if he'd missed something.

Taylor pointed at the monitors on which we'd watched Jill slip away to safety or death. We could still see the recumbent forms of various hell-princes and steam demons.

"When we begin our launch procedures," she said, "they are going to wake up. And then our principal goal in life will be to keep them from blowing us up."

15

"We'll do a cold takeoff," said Taylor. She seemed to know her business, but I didn't like the way she stressed that word, "cold." When I was a kid, the first strong impression I had from television was of the Challenger space shuttle blowing up. My parents had rented a documentary on the history of space flight. I remembered the white-porcelain appearance of the craft in the early morning. A frosty morning, the announcer told us. They'd never launched in such cold weather before. Some of the engineers, it later turned out, were concerned about icing. They were worried about certain wires.

The green light was given. The shuttle blasted off . . . and into eternity.

I wondered what our naval commander had in mind other than running a taut ship. She told us: "Normally we'd give the *Bova* a half hour of foreplay. A cold launch is when we start everything at once, flooding the engines with liquid oxygen. The risk is that the lox could pump through the lines so fast they'll crack. The good part of this risk is that the ship will be ready to launch in ten minutes. We are in the period of our launch window. The weather is on our side. The enemy is still asleep."

"Like you said, starting the ship will wake them up," I said.

"That's right, Taggert, and that's why we'll take only ten minutes instead of thirty to get ready. Those plug uglies down there are going to investigate. I'm hoping they're as dumb as they look."

"Yes, Commander Taylor," Arlene marveled, as awareness dawned. "They may think it's their guys in the *Bova*."

"Sure," agreed Steve Riley, joining us in the engine room. He was Taylor's radar intercept officer. Of course, he had to go through all that navy stuff with a superior officer before joining in the conversation. And they call us jarheads.

Riley had a neat little mustache, same as Hidalgo. It twitched a little when he became colorful: "By the time they realize we're not part of a scheduled bogeyman flight, they'll be toast from our thrusters."

"Even dummies might figure it out with thirty minutes to work in."

"So we don't give it to them," Taylor summed up.

"We could station a sniper in the hatchway in case they wise up," Albert said.

"Too dangerous," countered the skipper. "They might return fire."

"We're sitting on a Roman candle," I contributed. Suddenly I was very glad we'd sent Jill away.

"We have another problem, too." Taylor generously shared her apprehension with us—the mark of a good leader. "Along with passing up the luxury of a thirty-minute warm-up, I've decided not to use the start-up truck."

"What's that?" asked Albert.

"You probably saw it when you were sneaking in here. It's got a big plug the ship can use to get a charge for the blastoff. You may have also noticed that one of the cyberdemons is almost using it for a pillow."

"We call 'em steam demons," Arlene threw in gratuitously. (She probably doesn't think I know a word like "gratuitous.")

"I like that," said Taylor. "By whatever name, I prefer that it remain asleep."

"How can we take off, then?" asked Arlene, exchanging glances with me, her fellow expert on seat-of-the-pants rocket design.

Riley and Taylor exchanged meaningful looks as well—pilot-to-copilot looks, how-the-hell-are-we-going-to-make-it-work-this-time looks.

"We can start off our own battery," said Lieutenant Riley.

"I'm no rocket scientist," commented Albert and it took me a moment to realize our somber Mormon had made a joke. "But won't that drain the battery?"

"Yes, it will," admitted Taylor, "but not to the point of doom." It was funny how that word "doom" kept cropping up in everyone's conversation.

"It'll be like we were on a submarine," said Riley. That wouldn't be very hard for us.

"Run silent, run deep!" Arlene got into the drift.

"Yes," said Taylor. "We'll use a minimum of electronic devices in the ship. No radio broadcasts, no radar, no microwave. You'll be eating your MREs cold."

"What about light?" asked Albert.

"We have a good supply of battery-powered lanterns," Taylor said in a happier tone.

It didn't sound all that bad. I remembered the flight from Earth to Mars when they took me up for my court-martial. The trip was under a week. So what if we had to do it this time sitting in the dark most of the way? The trip might feel like an extension of our Hawaii vacation. There was nothing wrong with resting up before going through the Gate on Phobos. God only knew what we'd run into this time.

God only knew if we'd survive the takeoff.

The crew was the bare minimum, but it would do just fine for our purposes. It also meant there were enough acceleration couches for everyone. The *Bova* was cramped enough as it was. Along with the skipper and her copilot, we had Chief Petty Officer Robert Edward Lee Curtis and Petty Officer Second Class Jennifer Steven. Across the gulf of different services, we felt like comrades. We were the same rank. There were only three regular crew members.

Back to space for Arlene and me, though I never would have believed we'd voluntarily return to Phobos. I wondered what the chances were of passing by Deimos on the way to Mars, now that Deimos was a new satellite of Earth. Not our fault! We didn't drag it out of the orbit of Mars. We only hitched a ride.

As we neared the countdown—what do you call a countdown to the countdown?—I started to worry. I blamed my anxiety on my stomach. Many portions of my anatomy could make peace with zero-g, but my stomach would always be a stubborn holdout. When I finally admitted the truth to Arlene, I was speaking for my stomach.

One member of the crew, Christopher Olen Ray, was going into space for the first time, and the other guys were giving "good old Chris" a hard time about it. He couldn't have been older than his early twenties. He was worried about the g-forces of the takeoff. The first time is something to write home about. The way I look at it, that part is over quickly. Weightlessness lasts and lasts when some rich guy hasn't spent the money to keep your craft doing a full revolution so that you can enjoy the benefits of centrifugal force.

If this continued, I'd risk a good thought for the Union Aerospace Corporation. At least they were willing to spend some of their filthy lucre.

For better or worse, Commander Taylor gave the order to start the ten minutes that would feel like eternity. The old tub made a lot of noise when it was turned on. From my uncomfortable position on the acceleration couch I had a good view of a monitor. I saw the big ugly bastard right next to the ship wake up. Hell, the retros were noisy enough to wake me up. Hell-princes were so damned big that I found it fascinating to watch the thing fight the gravity to which we little humans are so accustomed. The ponderous minotaur stumbled as he got up, as if he had a hangover. I laughed. Doom demons bring out my mean streak.

Commander Taylor made sure that "all her babies" were securely fastened into their seats. This marine "baby" felt constricted by his safety harness. Then the ship started to quiver as it came alive, the fuel beginning to course through its veins. The vibration shook me in the marrow of my bones.

Suddenly I couldn't tell if the roaring came from the ship or the intercom, which was picking up sound effects from our playmates outside. Were they pissed off? Were they saying "Top of the mornin' to you?" (It was past midnight.) After all this time, I still didn't have a clue when these critters were happy or sad. A roar is a roar.

We had ringside seats, but there was nothing we could do if the monster squad decided to freak out.

The navy had its pet marines all trussed up. I didn't like the idea of playing sitting duck, but I understood that all we could do was stay put on top of our giant bomb.

On the screen, a large spider-mind scuttled over to the hell-prince. I didn't like that. If Ackerman's theory of broadcast intelligence turned out to be correct, it didn't change the fact that the spiders were the "smart" ones . . . and right now we needed all the dumb ones the enemy could spare.

Time was on our side. We didn't have that much longer to wait. I could hear Taylor and Riley running through the checklist. They spoke with the kind of precision that assured me we were in competent hands. I'd hate to die because of someone else's negligence. The little voice in the back of my head whispered that I had Viking blood in my veins, because I'd rather die with a battle-ax in my gut than fouled up by some numb-nuts who meant well but pulled the wrong switch.

As I heard the steady voice of the copilot announce, "Minus three minutes," I felt pretty good about the situation. These guys had a clue what they were doing, all right. Once we were under way they'd put on their oxygen masks and I wouldn't be able to listen in. Passengers didn't need to wear oxygen masks back where we were hog-tied, but there were emergency oxygen tanks in case the ship lost pressure.

I couldn't keep my eyes off the monitor where the big creeps were running around in search of some kind of authorization. That was why I was so happy to hear Riley say, "Minus two minutes."

"How you doin'?" asked CPO Curtis.

"Fine," I returned. I couldn't see much. If I

stretched my head at a really uncomfortable angle I could make out Arlene's legs.

"We're ready to weigh anchor," he threw back.

"Minus one minute," contributed the copilot. I was ready to believe we'd at least get off the ground. The monitor showed the return of the spider-mind as it pushed past the minotaur. The steam demon was close behind.

The intercom crackled with horrible screeching sounds—probably some alien code. It gave me a headache even before we lifted the *Bova* to greet the stars. The most inspiring part of the blastoff was watching the spider-mind get caught in the rocket's bright orange flame.

As quick as the commander could push a button, the demon guards were no longer a concern. Now it was the monsters of gravity and pressure that presented the obstacles. I felt them sitting on my chest. I'd been spoiled by easy takeoffs from Mars. Leaving the virtual nongravity of Phobos or Deimos didn't even count. I'd forgotten how much rougher it was to escape from the gravity well of the old mud ball.

It hurt. I had to reteach myself how to swallow. The pressure gave me the mother of all headaches. When I tried to focus on anything, my vision blurred. The vibration was outside and inside my head. Closing my eyes, I thanked the sisters of my Catholic school childhood for delivering Taylor and Riley.

We could watch our assent on television monitors. I would have preferred a porthole. But the resolution on the screens earned its description in the procurement file: "crystal clarity."

Blasting off when we did was like rising up into the endless night. Strapped to my couch, I could tell that the *Bova* was leaving the atmosphere only by watching the stars stop blinking. They were steady, white eyes spread out across the black velvet of space.

Arlene didn't think there was any poetry in my soul because I never talked this way to her. She'd been an English major once. I forgave her for that. What more could I do? She rated head honcho in this department. The best way to cover my ass was to keep poetic feelings to myself.

It was good to think about anything other than the physical strain of the liftoff. The boosters boosted. We shook, rattled, and rolled. I thought about how much work the commander and her radar officer must be doing without the assistance of ground-based support. No one to ring up on the phone and ask about bearing and flight plan. We were on our own.

The little voice in the back of my head chose that moment to raise an annoying point: what if the bad guys blew us out of the air? At no point in our discussions had anyone considered that possibility. Not out loud, anyway. Oh, well, as long as I was at it, I could worry if it might rain.

An old filling started to ache in the back of my jaw. Great, maybe I could find a demon dentist! The shaking was starting to get to me. Intellectually, I realized the ship was holding together. It takes a lot of power to climb out of Earth's gravity well. Emotionally, I expected all of us to fall out of the sky in a million pieces.

I went back to thinking poetic thoughts.

And then it was over. The *good* part was over. The vibration stopped. I noticed I was sweating like a pinkie after fifty push-ups. Then all the weight that I'd worked so hard to put on simply disappeared. Free fall. Falling. Zero-g. Zero tolerance for zero-g. My stomach started a slow somersault while I remained immobile.

Marine training to the rescue again! That, and the fact I deliberately hadn't eaten before playing space cadet. With applied willpower, I could put up with the rigors of space for the little week it would take to reach Mars.

Then the voice of Commander Taylor pronounced our fate. I heard it loud and clear. She wasn't using the ship's intercom. That was one of the luxuries we were giving up for this trip. But she had a loud voice, and everything was wide open so the sardines in the can wouldn't be lonely. Her words traveled the length of the ship: "We made it, boys. Now hear this. Reaching Mars shouldn't take longer than a month and a half."

16

I wonder which star in the sky is their ship. I may not be able to see it from this position, hiding behind an old Dumpster and watching monsters play. Their play is the worst thing I've ever seen.

Fly would be especially angry if he knew I'd already

thrown off Ken's schedule for my return. He'd scold: "Jill, how could you be so stupid? Every minute counts when you're using a timetable. That's why it's called a schedule, you stupid bitch."

No, he wouldn't call me a bitch. I like thinking he would. I'd like to think I bothered him enough he'd want to call me bad names. I'm calling myself a stupid bitch because I wanted to see the ship take off. I waited until it was out of sight. Then I went the wrong way.

I had a good excuse for going the wrong way. The monsters went ape when they realized the *Bova* wasn't supposed to take off. The spider that was fried by the ship's jets must have been important, because several other spiders showed up and wasted all the minotaurs in sight. They tried to waste a steam demon as well, but the thing was too fast for them. I never thought anything that big could run so fast.

While the monsters were busy killing each other I was able to slip away. Everything would have been fine if I'd been going in the right direction. As part of the plan, the navy guys left supplies for me along the return route. Ken planned the first leg of my trip to cover the same ground they followed on their last leg.

When I found myself at a convention of bonies and fire eaters, though, I realized I'd made a boo-boo. They didn't notice me; but I could see them clear as day. I wished the moon would go out so I could do a better job of hiding!

Some of the monsters naturally fought each other, but the bonies and fire eaters had a truce going. The same couldn't be said for the demon caught between them, one of the chubby pink ones Arlene likes to call pinkies. I couldn't help feeling sorry for the thing. The bonies—Dr. Ackerman called them revenants—were all lined up on one side in a semicircle. The fire eaters—also known by a really weird name, archviles—were lined up on the other side, completing the circle. A bonfire blazed between them.

The fire eaters could control their fire better than I realized. They'd send out thin lines of flame that would burn the pinkie's butt. He'd squeal. Fly always said the pinkies made him think of pigs.

The pinkie would jump over the fire and run straight for the bonies. They made a sound that was half rattling bones and half choking laughter. They couldn't use their rockets without spoiling the game. They seemed to have picked up a trick from human bullies on a playground. They used sticks to beat and prod their victim. One had an actual pitchfork he'd probably stolen from a farm. When the pinkie turned to run away from his tormentors the bony poked him in the ass with the pitchfork. If it hadn't been so sick, I would have laughed. But there was nothing funny about the pink demon finally falling right into the center of the fire where he grunted and squealed and died. I wondered if the bonies and fire eaters would eat him.

I wondered if they ate.

As they gathered around their roasting pig, I snuck away. If I could retrace my steps to the base and work my way around the perimeter, I might be able to pick up the route that Ken had mapped out for me. If I believed any part of what Albert did, and God was looking down, my only prayer was to get back on track. If the monsters were going to kill me, I wanted to be doing what I was supposed to before they ripped out my guts.

When Arlene gave me the big lecture about growing up and taking responsibility, she didn't say anything I hadn't already figured out myself. I could have said it better than she did.

Growing up was about dealing with fear. One night, when Arlene and Albert went to the supermarket in Zombie City to find rotten lemons and limes, Fly and I had a long talk. He asked me what I'd be willing to do in a war. He wanted to know if I'd be willing to torture the enemy, even if the enemy happened to be human.

I never stopped thinking about the questions he asked. When I disobeyed his orders about the plane and refused to fly to Hawaii without Fly and Arlene, I'd grown up. I wouldn't let down my friends. That's all there is to it. On the *Bova,* I felt they were letting me down. It was easier for Arlene to tell me she didn't want me coming along because I'm not trained than for her to say she loved me.

Fly and Arlene just don't know how to say they love somebody. Albert knows how. I'm learning how. I'll bet all the ammo in the universe that Fly and Arlene will never learn. But it doesn't matter. I love them. Even though they're gone, I won't let them down.

So as I look up at the night sky, wondering if they are one of the stars, I promise them that I won't get myself killed until I'm back with the plan. I'll be a good soldier. Just so long as I don't have to do the really weird stuff.

17

*"**B**ack on Phobos again—where a zombie once was a man!"*

"What the hell are you doing?" asked Arlene.

"I'm singing," I said.

"That's not singing," she disagreed.

"It's official Flynn Taggart caterwauling," I said.

"No, it's singing," said Albert, venturing where angels feared to tread.

"Are you making a wise move?" Arlene asked her would-be fiancé.

"Probably not," he agreed wisely. "But I recognize the song Fly has made his own. He's doing a zombie version of 'Back in the Saddle Again.'"

"Thank you, Albert," I said. "When I invited you to join the Fabulous Four, I knew I was selecting a man of exquisite judgment."

"That's not exactly how I remember our little adventure in Salt Lake City," Arlene corrected me.

I had the perfect answer for her: "Back on Phobos again . . ."

"Cease and desist, Flynn Taggart," she said, putting her hands over her ears. "We're not even on Phobos yet. Can't you wait and sing it there, preferably without your space helmet?"

"You can't fool me." I was firm. Besides, I'd already waited close to a month and a half—a lot longer than I'd originally planned on spending in this rust bucket. That had something to do with the fact that fuel was in short supply these days, thanks to the aliens, and something to do with the kind of orbit we were using, which made the usual one-week jaunt to Mars six times longer, which had driven me to singing. "We did not leave Phobos in shambles, like Deimos. There may still be air in the pressurized areas."

Arlene interrupted: "Along with pinkies, spinies, ghosts—"

"And a partridge in a pear tree." I wouldn't let her change the subject. "The point is that if the air's on, I can sing."

"The one weapon we didn't think of," Arlene agreed at last.

"Do we have any idea what the Phobos situation is like?" asked Albert, real serious all of a sudden.

"No," I said, ready to postpone my performance. "But whatever it is, it will be more interesting than one more second inside this . . ." I stopped, stumped for a good obscenity.

"In the belly of the whale," Arlene finished for me. She was getting biblical on me.

"I'm ready for battle," Albert admitted, almost sadly.

I took inventory of our section of the deluxe space cruiser, letting my eyes come to rest on my last candy bar. I'd used up my quota of Eco bars, the ones with the best nuts.

"Know how you feel, marine," I said to Albert. "We're all getting antsy. That may be the secret of preparing a warrior to do his best. Drag ass while delivering him to the war and he'll be ready to kill anything."

"With a song if need be," contributed Arlene. I'd found a new Achilles' heel in my best buddy: my singing voice. Maybe she had a point. I could just see a pumpkin deliberately smashing itself against a wall to escape from my perfect pitch. An army of imps would blow up a barrel of sludge themselves and die in glop and slop rather than let me start a second verse. Yeah, Arlene might have something there.

I didn't elaborate on any of this because our fearless leader chose that moment to join us. All the marines were awake on the bus. That was what it felt like—a bus.

The little voice in the back of my head could be a real pain in another part of my anatomy. It reminded me that this situation was strangely similar to a time in high school when three of us were the only ones awake in the back of the band bus—I was in the band; I played clarinet.

I was interested in a certain girl who happened to prefer a friend of mine. Her name was Noelle; his name was Ron. Bummer. But we had a nice three-way conversation going when our teacher suddenly came to the back of the bus. Old man Crowder. We called him Clam Crowder because he looked like something you'd pull out of a shell, and you wouldn't get a pearl, either. He just wanted to make sure that nothing was going on that was against the rules. The darkness of the spaceship, the kidding around of three friends, the arrival of the man with the rule book—all that was enough for me to be unfair to Captain Hidalgo. Time to snap out of it.

We no longer lived in a world of high school

football games. Now the pigskin only covered ugly pink demons who didn't need a rule book to spoil a day's fun.

I hadn't been able to stop thinking about Arlene's potential threat against Hidalgo, that she'd get rid of him if he got in the way of completing the mission. I'd never heard her talk like that before. I had known how daring she could be from the first time I met her, when she went at it with Gunny Goforth to prove she was enough of a "man" to wear her high-and-tight. I knew how smart she could be from Phobos where she left her initials on the walls for me, à la Arne Saknussen from *Journey to the Center of the Earth*, so I'd realize whose trail I was following.

Put smart and daring together and you have a combination that spells either patriot or traitor. I'd studied enough history to understand that it could be difficult to tell them apart. When your world is up against the wall, you have to make the tough choices. It's priority time. No one ever likes that.

Even if Hidalgo happened to be a martinet butthead he was still our CO. Whatever chances we had for a successful mission rested on his shoulders. That's what pissed off the dynamic duo of Arlene and me. I wanted Hidalgo to be good. I didn't want him to screw up. I wanted him to be a man I could trust, a competent man.

As I sat with my back to the wall, and watched the captain's profile as he chatted amiably with Arlene, I wondered what he would do if he realized how she felt about him. Maybe he'd shrug and just get back to doing his job. A man who does a good job doesn't have to worry about his back unless treacherous skunks are around. There were none of those under his command.

"Do we know which Gate to use?" Albert asked Hidalgo.

I almost answered. Had to watch that—chain of command.

Hidalgo answered: "You remember the director gave us the access codes and teleportation coordinates for one of the Gates." He smiled at Arlene and me. "You heroes need to work out among yourselves our best route to the right Gate once we land. Commander Taylor will get us as close to it as is humanly possible."

For a brief second I thought he was being sarcastic when he called us heroes. Arlene and I could be telepathic at times like this. The same thought flickered in her eyes. The next second the feeling passed—for me, at least. Hidalgo had spoken straight from the heart.

"You men," he said, and Arlene warmed up at that, "are the valuable cargo on the *Bova*." Same as the way we treated Jill as a case for special handling on the road to Los Angeles. "When we hit Phobos, I'll need the best intelligence you can provide."

"Conditions may have changed," said Arlene.

"Yes. Or they might be the same as when you left. Whatever they are, you two are better acquainted with the situation than any other humans alive."

I was glad that Arlene was participating in this discussion. "When you came over, we were discussing whether there'd still be air on the different levels."

"We'll wear space suits regardless," said Hidalgo. "If everything goes according to plan, we have no idea what's waiting for us on the other side."

"It's a mission of faith," Albert pointed out, and no one disagreed. "We must assume those on the other side will have the means to keep us alive. We can only pack so many hours of air. If we find ourselves under pressure we could save some of our own air for what's on the other side of the Gate."

"We'll be under pressure even if there's air," Arlene joked, reminding us about the doom demons.

"Maybe not," said Albert. "The devils may have abandoned Phobos Base."

"Sorry to burst your bubble, Albert," I said. "I'm surprised Arlene didn't remind you of what we discovered about the Gates. No matter what you take with you, you wind up naked on the other side. So you're dead right about having faith in the aliens on the other side."

"True," said Arlene. "That's been our experience. But we'd feel foolish if we didn't prepare and then found out for the first time that a Gate trip doesn't mean a strip tease." My buddy had a point.

"We've been lucky up until now," said Hidalgo. "We know the enemy has ships going back and forth between Phobos and Earth. The *Bova* uses a TACAN system, beaming out a signal showing them the bearing and distance of the ship. We may be the low-budget special, energy-wise, but we're not flying blind."

I hate flying blind.

"Are they using Deimos for anything?" asked Arlene.

"Not so far as the director and his team have found out. You two did such a good job of wrecking it that they may have given up on it."

"Outstanding," said Albert. 'Course he was looking at Arlene instead of me.

"We've been fortunate not to run into the enemy, but space is big, isn't it?" The way Hidalgo said that made me wonder if he was making a joke.

The next moment he did! "You know, Lieutenant Riley told me a funny one," he began. I noticed that he'd been pretty chummy with the radar intercept officer, but why not? Same rank attracts, especially between services. I'd hit it off with Jennifer, the PO2. I rarely called her by her last name.

Whatever the reason, it was good to see Hidalgo being human, even if we had to listen to his joke: "How can you tell the difference between the offense and defense of a doom demon? Give up? You can't tell any difference because even when we're kicking their butts, they're still offensive."

Discipline and duty pay off. I made myself laugh. There should be medals for this kind of service.

After the officer joke, Hidalgo left us alone. I was all set to resume my song, figuring anything would go down well after that joke.

Arlene headed me off at the pass. "Albert," she said quickly, "have you found any good books to read in the navy's box?"

"Lots of old books," he said. "The one I've read twice is *Bureaucracy* by Ludwig von Mises. He wrote about freedom when the only threat to it was other human beings. He said capitalism is good because it 'automatically values every man according to the services he renders to . . . his fellow men.'"

"No friend of socialism, is he?" asked Arlene.

Albert didn't hear the playfulness in her voice. He gave her a straight answer. "The book was written during World War II. He uses Hitler and Stalin as his two perfect models of socialism in practice."

Arlene was up on the subject: "They didn't kill as many people as the demons have, but not for lack of trying."

I contributed my bit. "Back at Hawaii Base I

overheard a female lab tech say what has happened is good for the human race because the extermination of billions of people has made the survivors give up their petty selfishness and band together for the common good."

"Jesus Christ!" said Arlene.

I noticed Albert didn't even wince any longer when she talked that way.

"Not everyone fights for the same things," said Albert with a shrug. "We do."

"Close enough," I agreed.

"Let's have a toast," said Arlene. "Something better than water."

"I have something," said Albert. While he pushed off in the direction of his secret stash (Paul had given him some good stuff), Arlene went over to her couch and dug out a book she'd been reading from the box. She'd always been very adept at maneuvering in free fall. I stayed put.

When she got back, I admitted, "I wish they had more of those magnetic boots so they could spare me a pair."

"The navy doesn't have enough for its own personnel," she reminded me. "Just be grateful we have a skeleton crew or there wouldn't have been acceleration couches for us."

"Yeah, tough marines don't need luxuries like a place to park our butts. We don't need internal organs, either. Just stack us up like cordwood in the back of the bus."

"Bus?"

"You know what I mean. What do you have in your hand?"

"*Cyrano de Bergerac*," she announced, holding a volume up. "I didn't expect to find my favorite play in

132

the navy's box. Since I don't have Albert's memory, I want to read you the ideal passage for my toast."

While she flipped the yellowing pages, Albert returned bearing gifts—a soup-bag. His big grin told me the content of the bag was anything but soup.

"Found it!" chirped Arlene. While Albert prepared the nipple we would all use to partake, she read to us: "'I marched on, all alone, to meet the devils. Overhead, the moon hung like a gold watch at the fob of heaven; Till suddenly some Angel rubbed a cloud, as it might be his handkerchief, across the shining crystal, and—the night came down.'"

She cleared her throat and said huskily, "May we bring down the eternal night of space upon the enemy."

As I took a sip of Burgundy wine, I felt that we were the Three Musketeers ready to fight the demon pukes . . . in whatever form they might take.

18

Fly was right. We were back on Phobos again, where a zombie once was a man. We didn't see any zombies this time. I was glad about that. They reminded me of Dodd. It's bad enough losing a lover the normal way without seeing him turn into a shambling travesty of someone I once loved. In my nightmares I still heard him calling: "Arlene, you can be one of us."

They say you can't go home again. But you can return to hell if you're crazy and you deliberately take a one-way ticket to Phobos.

The crew of the *Bova* had acquitted themselves admirably when it was time to deliver their cargo to the infernal regions. Phobos is so small that it's a real challenge to a space pilot. Deimos was a tougher port when it was still in its orbit around Mars. It was an unseemly rock covered by protrusions that could rip a ship if you miscalculated the angle or speed. Phobos was much smoother and rounder—more what we Earthers expected of a moon.

"How can they call something only ten miles long a moon?" Taylor asked as she did the painstaking maneuvers to rendezvous with Phobos. We were only a few miles away, matching orbits with the little black patch blotting out the stars. I counted myself fortunate that the commander had agreed to let me come up front to watch us "return." Our new pukehead friends kept joking that Fly and I were coming home. All the kidding may have made it easier to swing the invitation for Albert and me. He was as happy as a kid as we stood together in the hatchway and saw what the skipper saw.

There was no need to strap down when the gravity field of Phobos was virtually nonexistent. The artificial gravity areas produced by alien engineers had no effect on the rest of this glorious piece of space rock, especially not to Commander Taylor who had to do the stunt piloting.

Back in the UAC days, her job would have been a lot easier. The boys on the ground would send up a shuttle and bring us down without the ship even needing to land. Now the idea was to keep from being seen. There didn't seem to be any lights or activities on this side of Phobos. A good sign. I was hoping that if the moon hadn't been abandoned we might at least have reached it during a period when most of the bad guys were away. I wanted to laugh at the thought of a skeleton crew of . . . bonies.

The Big Four didn't need all this special attention. We were willing to hop down. Paratroopers of the Infinite! We could suit up and use mini-rockets to come in like mini-spaceships. With a bit of luck we wouldn't smash ourselves to a fine red spray—an appropriate death with Mars hovering over our heads, like the god of war.

Now for the first time Commander Taylor allowed herself to be testy with her marine passengers. "This is no time for a gung-ho kamikaze operation! The mission is a failure if you die before you meet what's on the other side of the Gate. We know how important your mission is and that the *Bova* is expendable. Why do you think we carted a few UAC goodies along just for you? Finding UAC stuff isn't easy anymore but you need every advantage. And remember that we will remain in this area until you return. If Phobos is too dangerous, we'll wait farther out. When any of you return from the mission, you will be greeted by someone . . . unless all of us are dead. Meanwhile, you will have the safest passage to Phobos that it is within my power to grant. Now not another word about paratrooping in."

She'd made such a big production out of it that I

took my chance for Albert to finally see a space skipper do her stuff; and I wasn't averse to getting an eyeful myself. The landing took a full hour once Taylor was in position to touch down ever so gently on the moon. I wasn't nervous, even though "Phobos" means "fear."

Hidalgo took command with grace. I was starting to feel more comfortable about him. I wasn't sure what had changed. He'd had us keep our gear in top condition aboard the *Bova,* but he hadn't been neurotic about it. Plus there was only so much exacting inspection he could do in the near-dark.

Hidalgo was beginning to assume his proper place in the pecking order as the fire team commander. The problem he had was that this position should have been held by the team member with the most combat experience. For this war, that narrowed down the list to two living marines: Fly and me. Next came Albert because he'd fought the monsters with us, close up and dirty. When Colonel Hooker saddled us with Hidalgo the test immediately became: is he an asset or extra baggage? I liked traveling light.

This was the last place for a know-it-all to try to assume command. Fly and I had the most firsthand information and we were still shooting in the dark most of the time. Hidalgo asked the right questions. He listened. Even though we'd never had the opportunity to train together to the point where we could operate as one perfect fighting machine, three of us did have this seasoning. With some applied intelligence, Hidalgo could be the brain.

Fly and I had worked out the route. Captain Hidalgo sent us in doing a simple echelon formation, with Albert taking the point. Then came Fly, then

Hidalgo, and I brought up the rear. I kind of liked it that my beloved and I were doing all the security sweep area between us.

Albert was a good marksman and he had a brand new Sig-Cow. He filled out his space suit better than the rest of us. We'd worried there might not be one to fit him, but the mission had been too well planned for that. Naturally, Albert's suit was at the bottom of the pile.

Seeing him from behind was like watching him grow in height as he looked up at Mars. The distant sun didn't illuminate the scenery too well, but the *Bova* would light our way as we searched for the right facility. Mars looked more orange than red to me; at least it did in this light. I'm sure that Albert would have loved it if it had been the color of a spoiled pumpkin—pie, that is.

It felt strange to deliberately reenter hell.

Half-normal gravity returned. The lights were on. My heart sank, and not from putting on weight all of a sudden. Since the gravity zones were still functioning, I figured the enemy must still be around. This conclusion might not have been entirely rational, though. The gravity zones had been operating long before the enemy arrived. It was possible the things couldn't be turned off. Call it woman's intuition, but I figured the red meanies would have trashed everything somehow if they didn't need it anymore.

The next second I was proved 100 percent right. I hate it when that happens. I saw the flying skull before anyone else did, zooming in at four o'clock.

Thank God we had our radios on. We'd discussed, and rejected, the possibility of maintaining radio silence for security and only talking by putting our helmets together. If we'd been that paranoid, the others wouldn't have heard me. In space they hear you scream only when your radio is on.

"Look out!"

Albert nailed the sucker before it could chow down on the material of his pressure suit. We hadn't had time to find out what currently passed for air here. The .30-caliber slugs did the job, and the skull skidded over to the nearest access-tube ladder. Down it went.

I wasn't the least bit surprised when a moment later Fly announced, "The test is positive. We can breathe the air."

"Remove helmets," Hidalgo ordered calmly. The suits were well designed for our purposes. The helmets hung in back, leaving our hands free so that we wouldn't be impeded while we added to the body count. Or head count, as the case might be.

"If everything's as we left it," I blurted out after my first gulp of base air, "we can expect a lot of opposition before we reach the Gate."

"Take it easy, Corporal Sanders," said Captain Hidalgo.

"Yes, sir." He was acting as if he knew his business.

"We'll handle them," he said. "That's why we're armed with state-of-the-art boom sticks." Another try at humor. This had started with his friendship with Lieutenant Riley. I didn't know how long it would last, but I kind of liked it.

Hidalgo gave the orders. We followed. Of course, the orders were based on our accurately locating the correct Gate.

We encountered no opposition for the next fifteen minutes. We did find a functioning lift that appeared to have been repaired with pieces of a steam demon. I didn't like the idea of using it but Hidalgo made the decision. Halfway down the shaft I could see through a ragged hole in the wall that the ladder I would have gone down ended in a tangle of spaghetti.

The makings of a reception committee waited for us at the bottom. If the skull had contacted them before we wasted it, they might have caused us some trouble. By this time, I thought I'd seen it all. I was wrong again.

Occupying the center of the room was an almost intact spider-mind. All that was missing was the head. In the smashed dome on top, where normally resided the evil brain-face, two spinies were doing something. They almost seemed to be laughing, and I could understand why Fly called them imps.

They were eating. When one of the imps looked up from his meal, I could see gray and red splotches on his brown face. Bits of gore dripped off the white horns sticking out from his body. Then he lifted one of his claws, and I saw what was dripping from it.

I was grateful Captain Hidalgo had ordered us to remove our helmets. I couldn't help throwing up, a reaction that surprised me. Why should my stomach churn at the sight of imps devouring a spider-mind? I'd seen far worse things happen to human beings and not lost my cookies.

I guess I'd reached a new level of disgust, though I didn't think there was anywhere lower. The imp saw us at about the same moment we saw him. Instinctively he threw one of his patented fireballs, but he forgot he was still holding on to a dripping chunk of spider tissue. The gory piece of bug brains caught fire, and the imp was scorched by his own flame.

By now the other imp figured out what was happening. He was smarter than his brother and did something I would have thought impossible. The spider's gun turret rotated in our direction and started spitting out its venom: 30mm rounds.

We would have been in trouble if it had been an actual spider-mind. But we had one of Commander Taylor's presents. While I zigged, Fly zagged. Albert and Hidalgo did their part by staying alive. The show belonged to Fly.

I never thought I'd see a BFG 9000 again, the crown jewel of UAC's weapons division. Three blasts would take care of a fully operational spider-mind. One blast proved more than sufficient for the imps who had themselves a great tank but weren't properly trained to use it.

"Praise the Lord!" shouted Albert.

"And pass the ammunition," said Fly, sweat beading on his forehead and a big grin growing underneath.

"Better than a chain saw," was my on-the-spot report.

"Regroup," said Hidalgo. "It'll be a shame to lose that fine weapon when we go through the Gate."

Albert tried for optimism. "Maybe we could leave it on the other side for when we return?"

"We could never risk that," answered the captain. "This place is crawling with vermin. We don't want them to get their claws on this weapon."

None of us said aloud the obvious: *If we return.*

The plan we'd made with the *Bova* was "no news is bad news." By now they knew we weren't alone on this rock. We'd continue observing radio silence between ourselves and the ship.

Fly summed up the situation. He's always good at doing that. "We've seen this place when it was crawling, Captain. Right now it's almost deserted. I don't have any idea why or how long it will last, though. It could be swarming again by this time tomorrow."

"Commander Taylor and Lieutenant Riley know the risks," he said, which struck me as a little odd. Seemed to me that the primary subject on the table right now was the fire team.

"Then we're enjoying good fortune," said Albert—a bit pompously, I thought. A problem I've always had when I fall for someone is that I become hypercritical. I think Fly has this problem as well.

Hidalgo gave us the word, and we moved on. I was astonished that I hadn't fired my plasma rifle yet. But it's wrong to wish for such things. I'm just superstitious enough to believe that you get exactly what you wish for.

My opportunity to test my weapon came with the appearance of a new monster. I hate new monsters. This one I mistook for a pumpkin. There were plenty of similarities: big round floating head, one eye, a gasbag with satanic halitosis.

The differences, partly obscured by a sudden change in the light, were most annoying. We might have become a little lazy. We had the best weapons, and the opposition was thin. Seeing a round thing come floating around the corner seemed almost too easy. One lousy pumpkin. Who was going to lay dibs on it? Who would have the pleasure of hosing it?

Hidalgo's reflexes might have been a little off, as well. He hadn't experienced Phobos when the shit storm came down nonstop. Even so, he got off a shot with his Sig-Cow. Some of the shots connected.

He'd succeeded in getting the thing's attention. It returned fire. I expected the usual: lightning balls. But this one had a surprise in its gullet. We were treated to a stream of flying skulls pouring out of its mouth, each one as nasty as the one Albert had shot out of the sky a short time before.

But now the sky was full of them.

19

The colors started shifting. That was a new trick. The corridor went from normal light to blue and then red, distracting us just enough so we wouldn't notice that this pumpkin was something other than a pumpkin. As its single eye focused on me, my only thought was that here we had a larger than usual pumpkin. As it vomited out the first flying skull, I still didn't understand what was happening. I had the dumb idea that it had eaten one of the smaller heads and couldn't keep it down. (Down what?)

As a second and third skull came zooming out of the ugly mouth, I started to read the picture. The first skull reached me before I could bring up the BFG. I heard Arlene shout, "Fly," just as I did the next best thing to shooting the little bugger: I kept it from taking a bite out of my shoulder by swinging around so that it collided with my helmet. There was a metal-on-metal sound as it dented the helmet and bounced off, making itself a perfect target for Hidalgo, who popped it.

Around about now we lost count of the skulls that filled the narrow corridor. It looked as if we'd knocked over a basket of candy skulls from Mexico's Day of the Dead celebrations . . . but there was nothing sweet about our tormentors.

Hidalgo froze for a few seconds. That was all. A brief moment of battlefield shock. If we lived, I could count on Arlene chewing my ear about it. And I could hear myself answering that we hadn't scored all that high in the reflexes department on this one. If we lived.

"I'll try for the pumpkin!" I shouted. The BFG 9000 would do the job—if I could just get a clear shot. The problem wasn't finding an opening through the skulls—the blast would pulverize them—the problem was to make sure that Albert was outside the field of fire.

Meanwhile, the others didn't need to be told to eliminate the flying skulls. No problem. There was only a zillion of 'em. Hidalgo proved himself worthy of command yet again. He didn't say a word. He was too busy blasting away with his Sig-Cow, taking down his quota.

Arlene provided Albert and Hidalgo with a helpful safety tip: "Don't let them bite you!" She shouted this over the sound of her plasma rifle. She almost took down the main problem with her first blast, which went through three skulls. But this particular pumpkin was smart. The damned thing floated back around

143

the corner where we'd first sighted its ugly mug. Then it kept spewing out skulls from its more protected position—a clever move, I had to admit.

Of course, the solution was obvious. I realized that I didn't really need a clear shot for the BFG if I could just see the target area. I blew away the entire wall and destroyed the ugly. Then, just for good measure, I pulled the trigger again. As the debris settled, I realized that I'd dropped half the skulls with those two shots, and the others were bumping into each other in the dust-filled air. This finally settled a question for me: the bastards didn't have radar.

The little voice in the back of my head insisted we were in too close quarters for using a weapon like the BFG. I couldn't hear anything else because of the ringing in my head, so I argued with the voice, reminding it that once upon a time I'd done a much crazier thing—I'd used a rocket launcher in an enclosed area.

The voice didn't have a good answer to that, and by then I could hear Arlene cursing a blue streak. She was bent over Hidalgo, her medikit open. Albert stood over the two of them, blasting the remaining skulls out of the corridor. I felt a little dizzy but managed to stumble over to rejoin the human population of hell.

At least one of the skulls had reached the captain and ripped up his throat something fierce. Hidalgo's torn space suit had a whole new meaning now: walking body bag. Arlene was doing what she could, but there was damned little hope for the captain. It looked as if we'd be finishing the mission sans officer. The way Arlene was feverishly working on Hidalgo it was hard to believe she'd ever talked about spacing his ass out an airlock. There's no substitute for being in combat together.

The last skull was either down or had flown the coop, but Albert remained on guard. I was grateful that the colors had stopped shifting, and I wondered if the light show had been part of this superpumpkin's powers. Whatever the facts might be, I'd become distinctly prejudiced against round things that floated through the air. They seemed to live in a permanent condition of zero-g. That was enough reason to hate them right there.

As we milled around helplessly, watching Arlene try to close the wound in Hidalgo's throat, I noticed Albert tense up. He raised his Sig-Cow to fire at something that was drifting in the air behind us. Naturally, I assumed it was another skull.

The last thing I expected to see this side of paradise was a blue sphere drifting toward us. A gorgeous, beautiful, welcome blue sphere. One of those miracles that had saved both my life and Arlene's. A blue sphere that Albert was seconds away from blowing to kingdom come.

"No!" I shouted, pushing his arm at the same time. Good thing I acted as I spoke. It was too late to stop him from pulling the trigger, but I spoiled his aim.

I couldn't remember if Arlene or I had told Albert about the blue spheres. It was pretty likely we had. But in the middle of a fight you don't expect the new guy to hesitate on the off chance it's not an enemy coming to say hello. It was only dumb luck I was saved the first time I encountered one.

Luck. Back to luck. How in the name of all the saints did this baby show up at the precise moment Hidalgo needed it? Arlene and I had just run across ours. This one was making a house call.

"It's a good one," I told Albert. "Like an angel. The blue spheres can heal us."

He lowered his weapon, and I gestured for Arlene to step back. Not one to waste a precious second, Albert reloaded. I moved out of the way, too. The blue sphere descended on Hidalgo, who wasn't the least bit worried; he'd blacked out from loss of blood.

The sphere burst the moment it touched him, making a popping sound like a cork coming out of a bottle. The color became darker as it spread, changing from sky-blue to a rich purple. Hidalgo was surrounded by a violet haze that became a glistening liquid on his body and then seeped through his pores. The ugly hole in his throat closed like two lips pressed together, and his face flushed as new blood pumped through his body.

A few minutes later he opened his blue eyes and regarded us with surprise. "What happened?" he asked.

Arlene did her best to tell him.

He gratefully sipped water from the canteen she passed to him. "Incredible," he admitted, speaking more slowly than normal. He sat up against the wall.

Albert continued on his watch.

"We need to move," I said, once again possibly usurping his prerogatives. I remembered how sleepy I'd been after receiving the treatment.

"Let's get a move on," he said, struggling to his feet. "How far do we have to go?"

"Only a few klicks," said Arlene.

We moved out, Albert leading the way again. Hidalgo, growing stronger with every step, asked the obvious question as his brain began firing on all cylinders again: "The blue balls didn't seek the two of you out when you were here before, did they?"

"No," Arlene and I said in stereo.

"Then why would this one deliberately come to my aid?"

We walked in silence. We had no ready answer. Only more questions. Then I had a thought. That happens sometimes.

"When it happened to me, it bugged the hell out of me," I told Hidalgo. "Even though mine didn't go out of its way to save my butt. There was an important piece of information I didn't have then."

Arlene smiled. The old lightbulb clicked on right over her head. "The aliens who sent the message," she said.

"Right," I continued. "It never made sense that our enemies would fabricate these incredible monsters and then throw in a few Florence Nightingales to patch us up. Now I know better. The blue spheres are not here courtesy of the Freds."

"The good guys sent them," marveled Arlene, the same thought taking up residence in her cranium.

"You were right to call them angels," said Albert.

Hidalgo nodded. "If that's true, then they must want all of us to make this trip." Unconsciously he stroked his own throat, where there was not even a scar.

We reached the Gate without encountering any more opposition. The creepy critters had been busy playing architect again. I should have expected something like that, considering how they were constantly altering the appearance of the different levels.

The Gate was decorated in a sort of late neo-satanic style. All they'd left out was gargoyles. If they wanted that last touch, they only had to look in a mirror. The basic addition appeared to be a huge stone doughnut jammed into the ground so that it formed a doorway with the grid right in the middle. All sorts of weird crap was carved into it.

The monsters had no taste at all. Guess that goes with being a monster. The dips had put two horns on top of this horror, one on either side of the "head." Adding insult to injury, they had placed two big stupid eyes on the semicircle of stone in relation to the horns so that even the dumbest grunt would pick up on the subtle idea: a giant demon head with the Gateway for its mouth.

I was prepared to laugh out loud, but I thought better of it. Chortling didn't seem like a very nice thing to do while a good friend was freaking out.

"Moloch!" Albert screamed. His eyes were wide, and he was foaming at the mouth.

As a top fire team, we still had a few bugs to iron out.

20

Albert was too good a man to lose his grip now. As his commanding officer, I couldn't stand by and let him dissolve into a puddle. The team needed a leader.

This was always a danger when taking command in a dicey situation. The survivors could bond too much. I had realized the truth of this when I stopped feeling suicidal. After they pulled me back from my own dipdunk and told me how the blue angel had saved me, I was so grateful that I said a prayer. I did this silently, of course. That way I know God heard me.

I could truly understand Gallatin's reaction to the sight of the graven image. My parents took me to a horror film when I was only six, one of the dozens of movies about the Aztec mummy. The monster didn't really frighten me; but the sight of young maidens being sacrificed by evil priests gave me nightmares for a week. Their idol looked like Moloch.

As I grew older, I began seeking out the image of Moloch. I found it in the old silent German movie, *Metropolis,* and it showed up in a frightening picture about devil worship. But I'll never forget how effectively it was used in the movie they used to make the transition from the old series, *Star Trek Ten,* to the new one, *Star Trek: Exodus.*

These strange creatures we fought were apparently able to crawl inside our minds and extract the most terrifying images from the human past. Fighting mirror images of your own nightmares had to be bad for morale. Sergeant Taggart and Lance Corporal Sanders were watching me as I watched Gallatin. Taggart started toward him, but I gave the order not to touch him.

"Gallatin," I said, keeping my voice low. "Snap out of it, marine."

He seemed to hear me as if I'd called to him across a vast gulf. His eyes were glazed. But he stopped making noises ill befitting a marine.

"Look," I said, pointing at the ground. "There are no human bones here. There is no fire in the maw waiting for human slaves to shovel in human food."

There was, in fact, a solitary skull staring at us with empty sockets, but even the blind could see there was nothing remotely human about it.

Gallatin calmed down. "I fouled up, sir!" he said in his old, strong voice. I was damned glad. If words didn't work, the next step would have been to trade punches. Gallatin was no coward. He would never cut and run. If he went nuts and stayed nuts, he'd have to be put down.

"This is the Gate," said Fly, checking his coordinates.

"Why do you think they dressed it up for Halloween?" I asked anyone who wanted to answer.

"It's what they do," Sanders volunteered, keeping her eye on Gallatin the whole time. I didn't blame her. So far, their feelings for each other hadn't interfered with the mission. If there was a time for her to blow it, this would have been it.

"Gives me the creepy crawlies," I admitted.

"It's Lovecraftian," added Sanders.

"Oh, no," said Taggart. "Just don't say it's eldritch."

If I hadn't returned from the dead, thanks to the blue angel, I would have put a stop to the banter. Normally I'm a stickler for protocol, but death had provided me with new insight. (Sanders said I was only near death, but I know better.) We weren't on such a tight timetable that we couldn't spare a few minutes. Up to this point, Taggart and Sanders had been our guides, but once we stepped through that portal, they would be no more experienced than the rest of us. No one had a clue what to expect. We had orders. Hope was allowed.

"I'd never describe that as eldritch," she threw back at Taggart. "I'd only observe the lurid shimmering about the base of the stygian masonry; and how overhanging our fevered brows leer abhorrent, arcane symbols threatening our very sanity with portents of an unwholesome, subterraneous wickedness."

"Well, okay," Taggart said, surrendering. "Just so long as you don't describe it as eldritch."

This moment of R&R was no excuse to lay off work. Since the Marine Corps had failed to provide us with eyes in the backs of our heads, I ordered a modified defensive diamond. Half of one. All four of us couldn't very well cover the four cardinal directions. Two of us had to prepare for the trip. Then we switched the duo.

My pressure suit was torn around the neck where the skull-thing had bitten me. Taggart's helmet was damaged but still usable; the dent in the side did not prevent his getting it over his head, and the faceplate wasn't cracked. The only suit likely to leak was mine. At my query, Taggart repeated his belief that the suits, weapons, and everything else not of woman born would not make it through. The preparations might be a waste of time, but I wasn't going into the unknown leaving anything undone. We'd be foolish to assume anything.

Making bets was another thing entirely. The odds were entirely on Sergeant Flynn Taggart's side. That's why I asked one last time what it had been like for him the last time he went through a Gate.

He reported: "I retained consciousness, sir. You don't worry if your equipment is still in your hands because you don't have any hands. There's no sensation of having a body at all. Then suddenly pieces of you come back. It's like you think of them and you're whole again; or maybe it's the other way around. Hard to tell."

"Were you awake and standing when you reached the other side?"

"Standing, sir!"

We'd covered the same ground before, but we weren't under attack at the moment. I liked going through the checklist one last time. And now our time was up.

I gave the command. "Move it, marines!" We humped into the mouth of Moloch.

At first there was a sensation of moving, of motion, a light drop, or a dropping into the light . . . but it's hard to see without eyes. We had no hallucinations, though. Our minds were our own. You can just say no to hallucinations, but you need a tongue to say no. Know what I mean?

ESTEBAN HIDALGO: Does anyone hear my voice? I hear it, but I don't have ears. You didn't say we could communicate while traveling through the Gate, Sergeant Taggart.

FLYNN TAGGART: Never traveled in a group before, sir! Arlene and I went separately on the Gate trip from Phobos to Deimos. The Gates are different from the short-hop teleports.

ARLENE SANDERS: You can say that again, Fly!

HIDALGO: I've never experienced either. Which do you prefer, Sergeant?

TAGGART: I'm not sure, sir! Anything that doesn't require using a stupid plastic key card to pass through a secret door is fine with me. Last time I was on Phobos, I really hated that.

HIDALGO: This is annoying enough for me, Sergeant.

ALBERT GALLATIN: I like being here.

SANDERS: Albert? You don't feel you've been sacrificed to Moloch?

GALLATIN: The opposite. This is wonderful. It's better than sex.

SANDERS: Well, I'll grant you it's up there.

HIDALGO: What do you think about that, Sergeant Taggart?

TAGGART: About what, sir?

HIDALGO: Do you think this disembodied condition is better than sex?

TAGGART: Nothing is better than a clearly delineated chain of command, sir!

HIDALGO: Is that sarcasm, Sergeant?

TAGGART: No, sir!

HIDALGO: I don't like this experience. How much longer do you expect it to take?

SANDERS: May I answer that, sir?

HIDALGO: You are both veterans of Gate travel, Lance Corporal.

SANDERS: Time has no meaning here.

TAGGART: There is no *here* here.

HIDALGO: I was afraid you'd say that.

TAGGART: Since we don't know how far we're traveling, or how fast, there is no way to calculate anything, sir!

GALLATIN: Permission to speak, sir?

HIDALGO: Tell you what. While we are in this whatever-it-is, we can drop all formalities. No one has to call me sir. Now, what did you want to ask me?

GALLATIN: If we encounter God, should we address him as sir?

HIDALGO: In case the answer is no, I'm more comfortable with dropping the formalities. Did you hear that, Fly?

TAGGART: Yes.

HIDALGO: You are good at following orders.

TAGGART: Yes.

HIDALGO: I'd like to thank all of you for saving my life.

TAGGART: It was the blue sphere.

HIDALGO: Perhaps you willed it to appear.

SANDERS: That's occurred to me, too.

HIDALGO: Strange to be brought back from the dead by a creature I didn't see.

SANDERS: While you were unconscious, you didn't see the face on the sphere.

HIDALGO: I was dead. I saw the light. The sphere had a face?

TAGGART: I wonder if any of our hosts at the end of this journey will have a face like that? It didn't look like any of the doom demons.

HIDALGO: Doom?

TAGGART: We call them that sometimes, after we found out the invasion was called Doom Day.

GALLATIN: Did you feel that?

SANDERS: Can we feel anything?

GALLATIN: I felt something warm. I feel as if I'm back on the *Bova* . . . weightless. Must have a body to feel that.

SANDERS: Wait. I feel something. But it's cool, not warm. I feel as if I'm in free fall, also.

HIDALGO: Maybe our journey is nearing its end.

NOT HIDALGO-TAGGART-SANDERS-GALLATIN: Your journey ended a long time ago. You wouldn't be having a conversation if you were in transit.

HIDALGO: What? Who's that?

TAGGART: That's not a voice.

SANDERS: It's not an identity—not one of us.

GALLATIN: Are you a spirit?

NOT HIDALGO-TAGGART-SANDERS-GALLATIN: We are the reception committee. You had a long journey, a long sleep. You are only now returning.

TAGGART: But we are experiencing what happens toward the end of Gate travel.

NOT H-T-S-G: No, you are remembering the sensations accompanying the transitional state. The journey is over. You have arrived. To reassemble, you must begin with your last memories. You must be aided through the psychotic episode.

HIDALGO: Psychotic . . .

TAGGART: Episode?

NOT H-T-S-G: The fantasy. The death fantasy. Do not concern yourselves. Reassembly *is*.

HIDALGO: If we have arrived somewhere, may we be informed where?

NOT H-T-S-G: Here the many meet and diplomacy greets. The True Aesthetic welcomes you. Sirs, sirs, sirs, sirs!

TAGGART: Something tells me we've been talking on a party line.

21

I've never been able to explain to Arlene why I'm so convinced there's a God. She lives in a world of logic and science. Mysteries bother her. They are problems to be solved; and she insists on a certain type of answer in advance. Her stubbornness only makes me love her more.

I'm not stupid. I realize the object hanging over my head is no angelic being. But lying on my back and watching the slow movements of the gossamer creature with flashing jewel eyes I feel a deep calm. The butterfly things that flutter around its flower-shaped head are attracted to the eyes, as I am attracted. The gossamer being eats the small flitting creatures.

This flying alien is no animal. It is a genius of its kind. But it pays no attention to me. If poor Dr. Ackerman had lived and joined us on this mission, he would have fulfilled his life's ambitions. The alien base contains a remarkable collection of geniuses; it was a sort of a galactic Mensa.

I haven't been able to find out where we are, but I'll keep asking. The only problem with this place is that most of the gossamer creatures completely ignore us.

That's one development I never expected—aliens who are simply bored with us.

The bad part is how their attitude rubs off. *I'm* bored with us. If this keeps up, I'll lose my desire to shoot things. Never mind what that means for my career in the marines. We Mormons believe in a warrior god, warrior angels, warriors, but there's not a single fiery sword anywhere in this whole gigantic habitat. What's a fella to do?

I know. I'll make friends with some of the natives. There must be *somebody* in this burg who'll show a new guy a good time.

"It's good to have our bodies again," said Arlene over a cup of H_2O and a plate of little red eyeballs. They weren't really eyeballs. But then, they weren't really red either.

"Not bad," I agreed. "I think I lost a few pounds."

"Fly, there aren't any extra pounds on you."

I shook my head. "Our vacation in Hawaii put a few extra pounds on the old carcass."

"Not that I ever noticed," she said in her friendliest voice. "You know, Fly, I feel as if I'm on vacation now."

So did I. It was hard to believe we were on an alien base God knew where. We were sitting at a table floating in the air between us. We were not in zero-g, but the table sort of was. I'd never sat in a more comfortable chair. It altered its shape to accommodate my slightest move. We'd taken our pills and were now enjoying the best human dinner available to us. The only one.

"Captain Hidalgo is not on vacation," I pointed out. There had been a problem with him. The strange entity we called a medbot had told us that Hidalgo's brain and body were not yet in harmony, but they would be. Whenever we asked the medbot how much time it would take for Hidalgo to be on his feet again, the eye of the robot seemed to wink at us, and the thing produced equations in the air. To be honest, I wasn't completely certain it was a machine, but Arlene insisted it had to be.

Arlene understood one statement, which put her kilometers ahead of Yours Truly. She said that in quantum physics there is no such thing as absolute time; there is only time relative to the location and speed of the observer.

I'd settle for finding out how much longer it would take for Hidalgo to rejoin us. There was no one I could ask about when Albert might come out of his mood.

Arlene seemed to read my thoughts again. Maybe in this place she really could. "Albert's not on vacation either."

"At least he's all right."

"Physically, yes, but I've never seen him in such a strange mood before."

"He told me he was meditating."

She shook her head. "He told me he was trying to communicate."

"That may be the same thing with these critters. We could spend the remainder of our lives attempting to adjust and never get anywhere."

I remembered coming back into my body. When we had eyes again, I saw the naked forms of Arlene, Albert, and Hidalgo. We weren't alone. There were aliens with us, but my reactions were off. I didn't even worry about whether the aliens had weapons or were menacing us in any manner. I'd undergone a change in perspective unlike anything that happened when I Gate-traveled before. I perceived the naked bodies of my fellow human beings with a completely new objectivity. I figured the difference had more to do with where we were than how we arrived.

I didn't feel desire for Arlene. I wasn't judgmental about the bodies of the two other men. I didn't feel any locker-room embarrassment or competition. But I wasn't indifferent. I was *curious* about the human body, as though I were seeing it for the first time. I felt the same way about the aliens, whose strange forms were suddenly no stranger than the fleshy bipeds called human beings.

The oddity of the moment was the medbot, who was all the reception committee we rated. It looked like a barber pole with an attitude. When Hidalgo collapsed, none of us rushed to his aid. We were still in that weird frame of mind, which I can describe only as objectivity. For the moment there was no strike team of marines.

The medbot scooped up Hidalgo's prostrate form, but it didn't tell us anything about his condition. The weird thing was that none of us asked. If the room had been crawling with spider-minds, our trigger fingers wouldn't have twitched; there was nothing to aim anyway.

Slowly we had found ourselves again. It was like returning to a house you'd left in childhood and exploring each room again as an adult. Only this house was your own body. As we became less alien to ourselves, the real aliens seemed stranger.

Arlene had the guts to make the first move. Too bad she didn't accomplish anything.

"I've always said you're the bravest man I know, Arlene. I was still staring into my navel when you tried to strike up a conversation with the . . . others."

"Well, you've always been a navel man," she said. Catching my expression, she added, "Didn't you hear the *e*, Fly? You're too much of a marine to fit into any other service."

Yep, we were back to normal. That didn't seem to be getting us anywhere in this galactic Hilton they called a base. Maybe we shouldn't be complaining. We were alive. The medbot had seen to that and had answered most of our medical questions. There were some questions it simply couldn't answer, though, about where and what and who and why. These were outside its field of competence. But I'd find someone to tell us where we were.

The medbot dodged only one question, when Arlene asked how come it spoke flawless English. "The English of this unit is not without flaw," it said fussily. When she came right out and asked how come it spoke English of any kind, it said, "Guild secret," and changed the subject back to our biological questions!

We had plenty of those.

"How do you think this food compares to MREs?" I asked Arlene as she chomped down on one of the little balls that looked like eyes to me but reminded her of a different portion of human anatomy.

"Heated or cold?"

"Cold, like we had on the *Bova*."

"Better."

"Hot."

She shrugged. "Close call. But I'm not criticizing the chef. We can eat this."

"The medbot says the provider of the feast wants to

meet us. And he's not really a chef; he's more a chemist."

She took another healthy gulp of water. We'd both become quite fond of water.

"I'll meet with anyone," she said, and I nodded. When she addressed the various creatures surrounding us at our arrival they had turned their backs on us—the ones who had backs—and wandered off. At first I thought we were being snubbed. But that wasn't it at all. The show was over. They'd seen what they wanted and had better things to do.

"Do you think the chef is one of the aliens who sent the message?"

"God, I hope so!" When someone as atheistic as Arlene invoked the name of God, I knew she was speaking from the heart. I felt the same way. What could be more pointless than traveling so far—and one of these damned aliens was going to tell me *how* far if I had to wrestle it out of him—and find no one on the other end who gave a flip?

"We know the chef helped the medbot work out the details of our body chemistry, so it's a safe bet he wants us alive."

The first thing we learned from the animated barber pole was that everyone on the base was a carbon-based life-form. For all I knew, there wasn't any other kind. So far, everyone we'd met was also the same on both sides of the invisible vertical line or, as Arlene would say, bilaterally symmetrical. I was grateful for two things: Earth-normal gravity and reentering the oxygen breathers' club! But that didn't mean we might not run into some other problems. Hidalgo sure did.

So it made sense that they'd kept all of us on ice, in

some sort of limbo, until they were sure we'd be all right in the environment of the base. When Arlene and I went through the Phobos Gate to Deimos we were traveling between artificial zones that were terrestrial-friendly. That was good news for us. When you're naked at the other end, you better hope you can breathe the air and your skin can take it. I was damned glad they could handle human specimens here. I just hoped Captain Hidalgo would pull through.

"Don't you like the food?" Arlene asked, noticing that I'd left half my meal unfinished.

"It's okay. The truth is, I'm not really hungry. My stomach spent so much time in zero-g aboard the *Bova* that it's taking its time returning to normal. Plus I'll let you in on something."

"What?" she asked, leaning forward conspiratorially.

"Practice makes perfect. They'll improve at making food for us."

She stretched like a cat. "Fine with me," she said. "Who would have thought the hardest part of keeping us alive would be feeding us?"

The medbot had sounded proud when it rattled off the information. Their first analyses had told them most of what they needed to know, but not everything. They knew we needed calories, proteins, amino acids, vitamins, but they did not know the proper combinations or amounts! The big problem for our hosts was figuring out how to synthesize the amino acids we eat.

This was a subject about which I was plenty ignorant. Ever since I started blowing away imps and zombies and ugly demons of all descriptions, my education had been improving. Fighting monsters must be the next best thing to reading your way through the public library. They both beat going to college, if I could judge from the usual butthead who thought he was hot snot because he dragged part of the alphabet behind his name.

The medbot was a bit technical in its non–flawless English but "Dr. Sanders" helped me pick up the basic points. The alien chef took some of his own food and injected it with human amino acid combinations. The first attempts were served to a high-tech garbage disposal. Arlene rambled a little about random combinations of four amino acids, then reached her climax.

The ropy things on the barber pole began to throb, and out of the top came a bottle of white pills, a present from the alien gourmet. We'd have to take those pills if we wanted to live.

The pills were blockers. While experimenting continued in the higher cuisine, the pills would increase the safety margin. Where had we heard that before? They would chemically block anything harmful. Without them we were doomed.

Naturally I wanted to meet our benefactor as much as Arlene did. We'd exhausted the possibilities of conversation with the medical barber pole. So when the medbot told us we could meet our favorite alien we were eager to tote that barge, lift that bale, swim the highest mountain . . . whatever.

The medbot's instructions were clear. "The next time you eat, stay in the place where you eat." So we did. We didn't have any important date to break. Arlene had tried to talk Albert into joining us, but his appetite seemed even smaller than mine. He was off meditating again. Seemed like brooding to me. I wouldn't call it sulking. Hidalgo was still under medical supervision. So Arlene and I were the ones who attended the great meeting between worlds.

"Look!" said Arlene, stifling a gasp.

The chef was coming. The chemist was coming. The alien who gave a rat's ass about us was striding up the silver walkway, and he seemed eager to meet us. We could tell from his very human smiles. Two smiles, exactly the same, because he was a they—identical twins moving in unison. They were more than twins. They were mirror images of each other.

Arlene started to laugh. I tried to shush her, but it was no good. "I can't help it," she said.

"Arlene, this is important. Put a sock in it."

"I can't help it," she insisted. "They look . . . they look like Magilla Gorilla!"

22

Alone. Silence. He drifted.

It was different than before; he had not been alone before. Now there were no voices. The last words had been a metallic voice complaining there was a slight problem. Now there was nothing.

Then there was sound. He heard her plainly. His dead wife was paying him a visit. Rita. She was dead. Sliced and diced by a steam demon back on Earth. She couldn't be here.

"Esteban," she whispered in the dark, as she used to do when she woke up before him shortly before dawn.

"You're not here," he told her. It was the first time he'd heard his own thoughts since he was cut off from the others and placed in this true limbo.

"You've summoned me."

"You're a dream," he replied morosely. "I don't want to talk to you. I want to meet the aliens."

"But I'm the alien, Esteban. The only alien you've ever really confronted."

"No, I've fought aliens. Red devils. Shot the grinning skulls and been ripped by their razor-sharp teeth."

"You felt my teeth first. Felt my lips."

"Go away. Leave me alone, you traitor. I must return to my men. To my men and Sanders. They need me. I must complete my mission among the friendly aliens."

Rita's voice was like a song he'd heard one too many times. "I was your friend."

"Never that. You were my wife."

She was sad. "You didn't try to be my friend. I thought you didn't love me. So I didn't want to have your alien growing inside me."

Anger filled his mind, and he was nothing now except his mind. Cold. Hot. The desire to hurt. To fire a chain gun. To wield a chain saw. To fire a rocket that would obliterate all memories of his marriage. The steam demon hadn't been able to do that.

"Please leave me alone," he pleaded. "I must concentrate on the mission. Discipline. Responsibility. Command. Must return to the team. Save the Earth. Destroy the enemy. Save . . . loved ones."

"Love," she repeated. "Part of love is forgiveness."

"You killed our—"

"Love."

"You murdered the—"

"Alien."

"You're—"

"Dead!" She shouted the last word. "Like our alien, I'm dead. You'll be dead too, if you don't open yourself to new experiences. You must know what you're fighting *for*. You can't just fight *against,* otherwise the blue sphere shouldn't have bothered saving you."

Hidalgo heard himself say, "I was bleeding to death. Why should I be saved and finish the journey only to die at the moment of success?"

He felt his tongue move in his mouth. He felt his throat swallow. He had a body again. Now if he could only find out what they had done with his eyes so he could open them.

"I'm sorry, Fly," I said, finally regaining control. After encountering so many terrible faces, I was shocked to see something so friendly and funny. I stopped laughing. But the aliens still looked like cartoon characters.

To describe one was to describe the other. The heads were large, like a gorilla's, with huge foreheads. The eyes were wide-set. The nose was cute, like a little peanut. Their hair was walnut-brown. They had a kind of permanent five-o'clock shadow, like the caricatures of the first president of the United States to have his name on a moon plaque: Richard M. Nixon. Their complexion was a yellowish green; maybe they had a little copper in their blood.

Their bodies were massive and looked strong. The arms were a bodybuilder's delight. They were longer than a human's; I'd bet they were exactly the right proportions for a gorilla. Then again, I might still be trying to justify my reaction; the forearms bulged too much for the simian comparison. They were exactly like cartoons—I thought of Popeye the Sailor and Alley Oop. I couldn't figure out how Fly had kept from laughing!

The big chest seemed even larger compared to the narrow waist. I couldn't help noticing a detail that Fly would probably miss: the tailoring of their clothes was first-rate. They wore a sort of muted orange flight suit with lots of vest pockets. Except for all the pockets, the suits were surprisingly similar in design to standard-issue combat suits, Homo sapiens model. Some of the aliens didn't wear clothes at all, or if they did, I couldn't tell. It was reassuring to find these similarities to ourselves in our new-found friends. They even had cute little combat boots so I couldn't check on how far the gorilla comparison actually went.

There was no doubt about these guys being friends. "Welcome to you," they said in unison. All that was missing was a reference to the lollipop guild. There was some serious English teaching going on here.

"Are you brothers?" Fly asked before I could.

"We are of the Klave," they said.

"Can you speak individually?" I asked.

"Yes," they said in unison.

I was good. I didn't laugh. While I was working to keep a straight face, Fly took command of the situation. He stood up from the relaxichair, which seemed to sigh as he departed, and touched one member of the dynamic duo.

"What's your name?" he asked.

"We are of the Klave."

He repeated the procedure with the next one and received the same answer. Then he followed up: "That's your race? Your, uh, species?"

Magilla number one looked at Magilla number two. I think they were deciding which one would speak so we wouldn't suffer through the stereo routine again. One of them answered: "The Klave R Us."

"How many?"

The other took his turn. "Going to a trillion less. Coming from a hundred more."

A general would like slightly better information. I joined Fly. He was on one side of them so I took the other, effectively bracketing them. Now we had a ménage à quatre.

I touched the one nearer to me and asked, "Do you have a name separate from the other?"

"Separate?" he asked. Apparently there were some problems with the English lessons.

"This part of we?" asked mine. I nodded.

They put their heads together. They weren't doing any sort of telepathy. These guys were whispering the same sentence. Sounded like a tire going flat.

Then they looked up at the same time. Mine spoke first: "After looking to your special English . . ."

"Americanian," Fly's gorilla picked up the sentence.

"We are giving ourselves to a name," mine finished.

Then we stood there like four idiots waiting for someone to say something. We'd succeeded in getting them to speak separately, but now they played sentence-completion games. What the hell, at least they gave themselves a handle: "We are Sears and Roebuck. We are your friend. We will take the battle to all enemies, and together we fight the Freds."

Alone. Silence. She drifted down deserted streets.

In the late afternoon the temperature dropped quickly. Jill put her windbreaker back on, but she was still cold. She didn't like coffee, but she was glad to have the hot cup in her hand; and she needed the caffeine. Swirling the remains in the Styrofoam cup, she looked thoughtfully at the light brown color that came from two powdered creams. But it still tasted bitter, just like coffee. At least she had managed to find food in the abandoned grocery store.

The sun was at a late afternoon slant, making objects caught in the light stand out from their surroundings. She was grateful she had sunglasses.

She was less grateful that she was lost. Something had gone wrong with Ken's plan. He'd talked the captain of the sub into meeting her, but only if she arrived on schedule. She hadn't. The sub was long gone by now. Captain Ellison couldn't be expected to endanger his crew any longer than necessary.

Left to her own devices, as usual, Jill worked her way back to L.A., where the first sight greeting her was a zombie window washer. The thing saw her with its watery eyes and began shambling in her direction, brandishing a plastic bottle full of dirty water. Jill was fresh out of ammo.

She hated to run, especially from a zombie, the very

bottom of the monster food chain. But running was a lot better than being groped by those rotting hands with the jagged yellow fingernails. So she hauled ass.

A normal zombie might not run very fast. This one didn't have the energy to do anything but curse. It wasn't until Jill was three blocks away that she wondered if maybe the creature really wasn't a zombie. The thought that some homeless person had been missed by both sides in the war made Jill's skin crawl.

Jeez, it was possible. The zombies might not notice a bum, especially if he'd been sleeping in the right garbage and had a sour odor on him. The big monsters might assume he was a zombie, and any humans coming through the area would think so too.

The idea made her literally sick. She threw up and covered herself in an odor like that of sour lemons, which would be useful if she needed to pass for a zombie herself. She looked bad enough. She hadn't slept in days. The circles under her eyes and the graveyard pallor of her skin gave her a living-dead appearance.

She didn't like the sick feeling in her gut. A drugstore sign beckoned. She went in, hoping to find something that would settle her stomach.

Jill wasn't so exhausted that she forgot to take precautions. She took out her piece even though it was empty. Always a chance she could bluff her way out of trouble if she encountered a human foe.

The first tip-off was the clean floor. An abandoned store would have been a disgusting mess, but this place was spotless. Broken windows had been boarded up. She felt like kicking herself that she hadn't picked up on so obvious a clue from outside.

Then she heard low voices. Unmistakably human. Not broken bits and pieces of language repeated without meaning. Whoever they were, they sure as hell weren't zombies. For one thing, zombies didn't listen to really bad classic alternative rock.

What sort of people were in enemy-occupied territory? They could only be guerrillas or traitors. She examined her surroundings more closely. The original contents of the store shelves were missing. She'd made a bad choice as far as her stomach was concerned.

Large boxes stood in place of a drugstore's normal stock. Shafts of light from the setting sun slid past the boarded windows and illuminated the box next to her knee. She looked inside and saw that it contained bottles of a nutrient solution made from hydrogen cyanide.

She almost whistled but stopped herself. It would be a good idea to find out if the voices belonged to friend or foe. She had a sinking feeling they were the enemy. This stuff could be used in the monster vats, or in some stage of the creatures' development.

She'd find out while there was daylight. For all of her adult accomplishments, Jill was little-girlish enough to tiptoe without making a sound. On little cat feet, she crept over to an air vent where she could hear the voices much better.

Two men were talking in the next room. She couldn't see them, but she heard every word, loud and clear.

"The masters say we will inherit the Earth," said the deeper voice.

"They've already taken care of the meek," replied the higher voice, snickering. He sounded like Peter Lorre out of an old horror movie.

Jill didn't need them to spell it out: these were human traitors. The real McCoy. These dips hadn't crawled out of any vat. She was shocked that these human bad guys couldn't come up with a better name for the Freds than "the masters." Really . . .

"I was at the general's briefing," said the deep voice. "He told us the resistance is so desperate they've started a propaganda campaign to convince people that the masters have enemies elsewhere in the universe."

"Yeah, I heard that, too." The other one snickered. "The masters are the only life besides us. They've told us. Except for life they create, of course. That's why we're so important to them; we're the only other intelligent life in the galaxy."

Jill had heard enough. Fly had often asked what she would do if she got a crack at human traitors. She'd wondered about that, too. Now she had her chance to find out.

Dr. Ackerman thought Jill was a genius. As young as she was, she already knew there was a reality beyond cyberspace, and that reality was just as important when it wasn't virtual! She had many interests—like chemistry, for instance.

While Tweedle*dumb* and Tweedledee continued stroking each other, Jill checked the contents of the other boxes. The enemy was using this drugstore as a place to stockpile . . . everything Jill needed to make cyanogen.

The traitors were still chatting and playing their lousy music, making enough noise to cover the sounds of Jill's makeshift chemistry set. They didn't even hear her setting up the portable battery-powered fan next to the vent. She combined the ingredients and started them cooking. Then she stood well back from the deadly cyanide gas, covering her mouth with a rag she'd found in the crate with the fan.

The last words she heard from the traitors came from the deep voice before it wheezed, coughed, and choked. "The masters say the Earth is the most important place in the galaxy to them right now," he said, "and we're in the center of the action."

As Jill left the drugstore, she looked up at the darkening sky. "You're on your way to Phobos now. After that you'll go so far away I'll probably never see any of you again. I did those two creeps for you. Good-bye, Albert, Arlene . . . Fly."

23

"**E**arth is not very important."

"Come again?" asked Arlene.

Sears and Roebuck didn't pick up on her hurt tone. They were simply answering my question with unfailing honesty. I wondered if all the Klave were like this.

"They're not passing value judgments, Arlene," I said. "If the facts offend our pride, it's not their fault."

If looks could kill, my best buddy would have fried Fly on a stick. "Don't patronize me," she said—which was the furthest thing from my mind. "I was surprised, that's all. Why would the Freds produce a ton of damned monsters and flood our solar system with them if Earth is not important?"

"Don't ask me, Arlene. Ask them."

We turned to Sears and Roebuck. They said nothing. So Arlene carefully repeated her diatribe for them. Boy, did they have an answer.

"Earth is skirmish-zoned. They don't care go to humans. Galaxy is setting for whole game. You'd call galactic diplomacy by other means. No war goes to Earth. Your space is too small. Earth is move in game. All are having you here because you matter. All parts matter to the Klave. Whole game matters to the . . ." He used a word to denote the Freds. There was no English equivalent, and a Klavian word slipped in. To human ears, it was noise.

"Is it only the Klave who fight the Freds?" asked Arlene. Sears and Roebuck understood well enough when we spoke of the enemy. For whatever alien reason, they didn't call them Freds. I hoped I could persuade them to start using all our words if only so I wouldn't have to listen to a sound that put my teeth on edge.

In answering Arlene, they used another nails-on-the-blackboard sound to describe the larger group of aliens of which the Klave formed only a small part. "All here are opposed to %$&*@@+."

"Please," said Arlene, "could you call them Freds? That's a word we can understand."

"Freds," said our new pal.

"See, that didn't hurt." I thanked them.

"Sears and Roebuck are real gentlemen," said Arlene.

S&R smiled. It was great finding aliens who could smile even if it happened to be their version of a frown (for all we could tell). We didn't ask. We didn't want to mess with it. They were in there pitching. They made another noble attempt in their peculiar English to give us an education in galactic history.

I never dreamed there was so much going on behind the attack on humanity. Suddenly the zombies, imps, demons, ghosts, flying skulls, pumpkins, superpumpkins, hell-princes, steam demons, spider-minds, spider-babies, fatties, bonies, fire eaters, and weird-ass sea monsters all seemed trivial in the grand scheme being laid out for us. The monsters we fought were bit players. And why not? Humanity was a bit player in the galactic chess game being played out by the Freds and the message aliens.

And suddenly it was clear why we hadn't been greeted by a brass band and presented with a key to the city when we arrived. We were not big time. But it was also evident why we had been invited. We were in the bush leagues, but at least we were in the game.

Turned out it wasn't only the old mud ball that didn't rate star treatment. There were a lot more important bases than this one. I shook my head. I was just a poor old Earth boy on his trip to the big burg. This was the galactic base to me, even if it happened to be in the boondocks.

When I told Sears and Roebuck how I felt, they looked at each other as if they were checking out a reflection in a mirror. Then they said, "You will be informed soon-time about location. You won't go to boondocks, in your words."

They returned to their main theme. Once again I was impressed that the Klave seemed concerned about all life victimized by the baddies. So it made sense that we did rate special treatment from Sears and Roebuck. They were the most noble aliens on this whole colossal alien base, but they looked as if they'd just stepped out of a kid's cartoon.

A cartoon I had somehow missed when I was growing up. Arlene was younger than I was, but she'd seen a lot more popular entertainment. She asked me why I was so culturally deprived. I knew how to shut her up: "I was busy preparing mentally, physically, and spiritually for my role as cosmic savior. I had no time to waste time on frivolous media entertainment." That showed her.

I couldn't wait to find Albert and tell him the good news. As soon as Captain Hidalgo was on his feet again, he'd have to be briefed. Our mission was a success, after all. We'd found aliens who didn't want the Freds to occupy our solar system. It might not mean any more to them than a village or town in one of Earth's major wars, but we at least counted at that level. We rated Third World treatment by superior beings.

The little voice in the back of my head suggested that Director Williams would be more amused by this discovery than either Admiral Kimmel or Colonel Hooker would be. Hell, I'd like to see the faces of the human sellouts if they heard where they rated in the cosmic scheme of things.

Then that old mind reader Arlene asked S&R the googolplex-dollar question: "So what are you guys fighting about?"

An hour later, by Earth standard time, we still hadn't grasped what S&R were trying to get across. Their odd syntax wasn't the problem. We weren't picking up on the concepts.

We finally received assistance from an unexpected quarter: Albert joined us; he came swimming through the air. Not really, of course. It only looked that way. The base had gravity zones and free-fall areas. Whatever the Freds could do on Phobos, the message aliens could do better! Albert was simply taking the escalator. He had drifted up near the ceiling of our section. Then he slowly drifted down on a transition-to-gravity escalator! That's what it was. He moved his arms and legs as if he were doing the breast stroke, grinning at us the whole time.

I hoped he was over his sulk or pout or whatever it was. I didn't buy the meditation bit. He seemed eager to rejoin his buds. And he'd picked a good moment to meet Sears and Roebuck.

The moment Albert touched down, he took out a little purple ball and squeezed it. A duplicate of Albert appeared. I'd seen those toys before. We thought we had virtual reality on the old mud ball. The doppelgänger matched Albert's movements perfectly.

"What's this about?" I asked.

"Trust me," he said. "I'll tell you later." For the rest of the time he was with us, his three-dimensional image aped his movements a few feet away.

Arlene shrugged. So what if Albert was playing games to deal with his boredom? She made the introductions: "Sears and Roebuck, I'd like you to meet another member of our team."

The Magilla Gorilla faces grinned more widely than I thought possible. Looked as if their heads were in danger of splitting open. "We encountered these unit in times going before," they said.

Well, I'd be dipped in a substance they recycled very effectively here at the alien base. I may have judged Albert's meditations too harshly. He waved at S&R, and both of them waved back.

"We're discoursing the wordage but not reaching home plate," said S&R.

Albert helped himself to a glass of water from our table. "You must have asked them for background," he said.

Arlene playfully pulled at Albert's sleeve. He seemed very comfortable in the shimmering robes he'd selected. The designs looked slightly oriental to me. "Have you talked to them before?"

"Yes."

"Do you understand what the war is about?" she asked.

Albert sat in one of the chairs we'd vacated. "Near as I can make out, they're having a religious war."

S&R had mentioned diplomacy. It would have been nice if that word had registered on Arlene. She snorted when Albert said the *r*-word. "I'd expect that from you," she said with disdain.

"Arlene!" I jumped in.

"It's all right, Fly," Albert jumped right back. "I can understand why Arlene would react that way."

"Excuse me," she interjected, but despite the words she didn't sound polite. "Please don't talk about me in the third person when I'm right here."

Albert wasn't in a mood to back off. "We've been doing that with Sears and Roebuck, and they're right here."

The man had a point. S&R politely waited for one of us to address them directly. Otherwise, they didn't budge and didn't make a peep.

Albert regarded Arlene with a strong, steady gaze I'd never noticed from him before. I definitely needed to rethink my views on meditation.

"Arlene," he began softly, "it might not be possible

for us to understand why these advanced beings are in conflict. They have such advanced technology and powers that they can't possibly need territory or each other's resources. The war is some sort of galactic chess game. It may not be possible for us to grasp the root reasons for the war. I think the best we can hope is to make a good analogy. With my beliefs, the best I can do is compare the situation to two different branches of the Southern Baptists, or, say, the Sunni Muslims and Shiite Muslims. From the inside, there is a huge chasm. From the outside, the distinctions may seem insignificant. If you find my analysis unacceptable, we will say nothing more about it, but I would like basic courtesy, if possible."

For the first time in their relationship, Albert gave it to my best buddy good and hard. At least, it was the first time I ever noticed. Albert allowed himself to use a patronizing tone. I thought Arlene had it coming.

Apparently so did she. "I'm sorry, Albert," she said. "Your explanation helps. You know how impatient I am, but that's no excuse to be rude."

"Thank you," he said.

This seemed like a good time to pick up the ball and run with it. "Sears and Roebuck," I addressed them.

"Yes?" they replied.

"Did any of the conversation we just had help, uh, clarify the problem? Unless you weren't listening, that is. We weren't trying to have a private conversation right in front of you."

"Private?"

"Well, you know what I mean. Private! I mean, you have such a large English vocabulary . . . however you picked it up."

"Free-basing," they said. We all did a big collective

"Huh?" So they tried again: "Data-basing. We draw on large dictionary stores. Private is the lowest rank in the Earth army."

"Yes, well," I floundered around. "We'll return to that subject at a later time." I stared at their comic faces. They stared right back. "I've forgotten what I asked you," I admitted.

"Religion unclear going to object-subject," said Sears and Roebuck. "We are sorry we fail the exporation."

"Explanation," I corrected them without thinking about it. Jesus, I was becoming used to their sentences. "I don't mean to criticize you," I continued, "but we're not getting anywhere. Thanks for trying to explain."

"Criticize," said S&R. "Movie critics. Book critics. Art critics. Science-fiction reviewers . . ."

Albert saw the direction before I did. "Is that it?" he asked, eagerly. "Do you have aesthetic differences with the Freds?"

"War going on to hundreds of thousands of years," said S&R. "Go to planetary systems change. Different races are subjects, objects."

"How did it begin?" asked Arlene, suddenly as enthusiastic as Albert.

"You call them books," said S&R. "The Holy Tests."

"Texts," I did it again, almost unconsciously.

"Texts," they said. I felt like giving them an A-plus. "Books are twelve million years old. The Freds disagree with us."

"With the Klave?" I asked.

"All of us. Not only Klave-us, but all that are *here* us. We bring you for going to the war."

"Literary criticism," marveled Arlene. I wasn't

about to forget that she'd been an English major for a while.

Albert clapped like a little kid who'd just been given the present he always wanted—understanding. "The two sides are literary critics, conquering stellar systems to promote their own school of criticism. I love it. It's too insane not to love. What is their primary disagreement over the twelve-million-year-old books?"

S&R gave us one of their best sentences: "The Freds want to take the books apart."

Arlene screamed, but it was a happy kind of scream. "Oh, my God," she said, "they're deconstructionists!"

24

"**Y**ou'll have to fill me in on what that means," Fly whispered in my ear.

I was still reeling from the implications of what I'd blurted out. I looked at Fly with the blankest stare in my repertoire. "You mean deconstructionism?" I asked.

"Yeah."

I wasn't about to admit to the great Fly Taggart that I had very little idea. I didn't complete my college work. I was afraid that if I started collecting degrees in the liberal arts it would handicap me for life in the real world. But I'd picked up a few buzzwords. Time to bluff my way through.

"Deconstructionism is what it sounds like," I said. "Professors of literature take apart texts and examine them."

"How's that different from what other professors do?" Fly wanted to know. He was so prejudiced against the typical product of our institutions of higher learning that I wondered why he was pumping me at all. I'd become the official exception to his belief that college damaged the mind.

One more comment and I'd exhaust my store of information on the subject: "Well, they come up with different meanings than the authors intended." I'd shot my bolt. Before Fly could ask for elaboration and examples, I threw myself on the mercy of the aliens. "I'm sure Sears and Roebuck can take it from there," I said, "with all the information about our world they're carrying in their handsome heads."

"Nice try," said Albert as he endeavored to keep a straight face. I wouldn't put it past him to know plenty about the subject, but I'll bet he was still sore about my sarcasm earlier. Dumb Arlene! Dumb. Besides, what we really needed to know was what was in those old books, if we could understand them at all.

Sears and Roebuck did not rescue me. Their heads were full of information about our language, but they had a talent for confusion at the most inappropriate times. Like now.

"Deconstruction," they said, "is the article 'de' preceding the noun, 'construction,' as in deconstruction of a house."

Great. They were doing a Chico Marx routine! Fly

and Albert both lost it about then and broke out laughing. Well, if they could laugh at Magilla Gorillas, so could I. Our alien buds didn't join in, but I don't think they were offended. They didn't understand our humor. Not surprising, really. Humor is the last part of a culture to be internalized by an outsider, if even then. If there was such a phenomenon as Klave humor, we were just as unlikely to pick up on it.

Albert came to the rescue. I wondered how much time he'd spent with S&R while I thought he was off brooding. He made it simple: "We're talking about a literary theory. The Freds have one. Your side has another. If you look up deconstructionism in a history of literature you will probably find an opposing theory that might describe your side in this galactic war."

With a little nudge in the right direction, S&R could work wonders. "Justice a minute," they said. "We learn with going to photogenic memory. Deconstruction is not what we said. We understand the differential."

It was my turn to whisper in Albert's ear. I wanted to be friendly with the big lug and make sure I was forgiven. "I can't decide if Sears and Roebuck are harder to understand when they think they understand us."

"Amen," he said. I was at least half forgiven.

"We know what the Klave are being in the war," said S&R.

The suspense was killing me, even if Fly's eyes were beginning to get that special bored look right before he started rocking and rolling.

"You are what?" I prompted S&R.

"We are hyperrealists," they said. "We leave books together."

"And you leave worlds alone," Albert finished, pleased at the direction our conversation had taken.

S&R were on a roll. "When your unit is restored, we go to Fred invasion base and continue your part in the war. We will fighting with you."

It took a moment for me to realize what they were talking about. Our unit included Captain Hidalgo. I'd never thought we'd travel these incredible distances only to pick up two new members for our fire team. I wondered how Hidalgo would deal with this development.

"How far away is this base?" asked Albert.

I almost chided Albert but caught myself. How could we ask the distance to the Freds when we didn't know where the hell we were? I couldn't understand the reluctance of the aliens to give us the straight of it. Could Albert be trying to trick S&R into revealing our location?

Whether intended or not, that was the result. "The Fred base is two hundred bright-years away," they said.

"Light-years," Fly corrected them. If he kept this up, he might have a great career ahead of him . . . as an editor!

I figured it was my turn. "That doesn't tell us how far the Freds are from our solar system."

S&R answered immediately: "Two hundred light-years."

While I marveled at another passable reply from our hosts, Fly picked up on the content. "Excuse me," he said in his I-really-can't-take-any-more-surprises voice. "What did you just say?"

S&R said, "Two hundred light-years."

"That's the distance from *this* base?" Fly asked.

S&R nodded. They'd at least picked up one of our human traits. "The distance from *our* solar system?" he nailed the coffin shut. They nodded again.

Fly sounded so calm and reasonable that I feared for all of our lives. This was worse than when he found out about the month and a half of travel time on the *Bova*.

"Just so I'm absolutely clear," he said, "regarding the location of this galactic base, we are located exactly *where?*"

If Sears and Roebuck had seemed like cartoon characters before, the impression was even more pronounced now. There was one word they had apparently missed in their extensive study of the English language: "oops."

S&R didn't hold back any longer: "We are past the orbit of Pluto-Charon."

"Why didn't you tell us this before?" I asked.

"Need to know," they said. "Hidalgo part of your unit will be returned to you soon, and unit completes all."

"It was getting about time to tell us anyway," Albert translated helpfully.

"Let me get this straight," said Fly, oblivious to all other subjects until he was satisfied on this one. "We've been convinced of the relative unimportance of the Earth in the big scheme of things. So it comes as a shock to learn you have this space museum parked just outside our insignificant solar system."

I thought Fly was laying it on a bit thick. I would have told him to take a stress pill and calm down . . . if we'd had any stress pills. S&R didn't seem clued in to human frustration.

When Fly calmed down, S&R attempted to explain.

One thing I'll say for my pal, when he finds out he's been off the wall on something, he takes his medicine like a trooper. Hell, like a marine.

Naturally, we all believed we'd traveled many light-years to get to this base. Nope. Wrong about that. We thought it a strong possibility that we'd been in transit for many years, Earth standard time. Nope. Wrong again. Several other assumptions were shot down in flames as well. I remembered the director saying there was no way to pinpoint the location of the secret base, and I recall Jill teasing him about that. How desperately Warren Williams wanted to unlock the secrets of the stars.

The poor man would probably be as disappointed as Fly to learn that there is no such thing as faster-than-light travel. Many people have never imagined otherwise, but most of them would not imagine a galactic war with a myriad of alien races either. Up to this moment on the gigantic galactic base—which happened to be parked in our own backyard—I would have thought a galactic war *must* prove the existence of FTL.

I'd grown up reading all of the great SF writers. E. E. Doc Smith and his inertialess drive. John W. Campbell Jr. and a dozen clever ways to get around Einstein's speed limit. Arthur C. Clarke with a bag of tricks the others had missed. The discovery of a galactic war without faster-than-light travel blew my mind more completely than the spider-mind carcass Fly and I had plastered all over Deimos.

S&R finally succeeded in explaining the reality to us. Fly wasn't even all that much of a science-fiction fan, and he took the news really hard. It must have been all those *Star Trek* shows that not even he could have missed seeing. Or maybe it was just his romantic sense of adventure. We felt as if we'd traveled across the universe, and then we find out we're next door to the old neighborhood. Albert didn't seem bothered at all. There are no articles of faith about FTL outside of science-fiction conventions.

It was hard work extracting facts from S&R, but they were ready and willing if we were. Reality was like this: first of all, there is no such thing as hyper-space. Hyper kids like Jill, yes. Space, no. Everything happens at relativistic velocities. When we went through the Gate on Phobos, the trip took us almost seven and a half hours by Earth standard time, traveling just under light-speed as beams of coherent, self-focusing information.

The galactic chess game stretched out over millennia. We hadn't asked yet, but I was ready to bet the farm that some of these suckers lived a freakin' long time. It almost had to be that way. Otherwise how could individuals maintain interest in their blood-drenched games?

It had taken the Freds more than two hundred of our years to reach Earth in the beginning! This was my idea of long-range planning. This was my idea of an implacable foe.

These guys got off by critiquing twelve-million-year-old books and fighting over which important commentator correctly interpreted them! Jeez, I wondered how many alien races had been exterminated because of a bad review? At times the struggle had erupted into full-scale warfare. It didn't make Fly, Albert, or me feel any better to learn that now was a relatively calm period with only occasional brush wars along the borders.

Millions of rotting human corpses were almost overlooked. The monsters sent by the Freds to either end or enslave mankind were just one more move in the lit-crit game. As we painfully pieced together the story of life in the galaxy, I had the weird feeling that the Freds took the human race more seriously than any of the "good guys." Oh, we'd connected with S&R. Maybe the entire Klave operated at their high level of ethics and decency. But even so, the best we could expect from our allies was a chance to be marines again.

The Freds had sent hundreds, thousands, maybe millions of their demonic monsters to clean humanity's clock. Simple human pride made me feel for the first—and I hoped the last—time that the Freds were a worthy foe. They must be scared of us. The deconstructionists thought we might deconstruct them. The hyperrealists were busy with their own shit.

25

"**I** love you."

Arlene touched my face and said, "You didn't have to do this."

I thought I'd never get her alone. Then Fly obliged

me by wandering off with Sears and Roebuck. They were still trying to explain to him why we exist in a sub-light Einsteinian universe. Arlene was too depressed to want to hear the details just now.

Besides, I could turn off my Albert-projector right now. It was disconcerting to watch myself. I wasn't all that vain, and I didn't want to watch myself all the time. Of course, I'd had a very good reason for bringing the device. I'd spent time with S&R first and picked up a lot about their peculiarities. I could tell Arlene and Fly about that later. Shop talk. Business. The mission.

Meanwhile, something more important concerned me: my opportunity to be alone with Arlene! Our little spat was forgotten as she held up her gold ring. I think I saw the hint of a tear in a corner of her eye. The ring was attached to a necklace.

"How did you manage this?" she asked. The original ring had vanished along with everything else when we went through the Gate.

"Sears and Roebuck," I said. "We couldn't ask for better guardian angels."

She nodded in acknowledgment. "How much time did you spend with them before Fly and I met them?"

"Enough."

She chuckled. "You don't like giving away the details of your surprise."

"You can figure it out. Sears and Roebuck have more tricks up their sleeves than only synthesizing food for us. They synthesized the ring when I asked. I only had to give them the details. I didn't ask for a new set of dog tags."

"I'll live. Tell me, did you make any attempt to distinguish Sears from Roebuck?"

"Didn't seem worth the trouble."

"I know what you mean. Did you ask them to keep the ring a secret until you could surprise me?"

"No. Once they made the ring, they gave it to me. Now it was my business. Besides, I'm not sure they'd be very good at keeping secrets. They don't seem to have a privacy concept."

"I was wondering about that. I don't think they understand our concept of individuality, either. The Klave sounds like a collectivist society."

"Or more than that," I added.

"Yeah. I wonder how far the collectivism goes. It would be interesting to find out."

She stopped, waiting for me to say something. I merely regarded her and listened to my heart beat. Then I deliberately looked away. We were standing close together over by the rail next to the floating table. Overhead an aquarium drifted, the sea creatures within swimming lazily. My soul felt a great peace. I was finally witnessing strange things from other worlds, and I didn't have to destroy anything. I didn't have to take out the trash. I didn't need to fire a rocket overhead and spill fish guts all over my lady love.

I was tired of shop talk. I waited for Arlene to bring the subject back to *us*. The ring did it. Her eyes went from mine down to the gold circle in her hand and then back up again.

"This means the world to me," she said. "The universe." She said it as if she meant it.

I wished she had long hair instead of a high-and-tight. Hawaii Base had a barber, dammit! With long hair, a strand would occasionally fall into her eye and I could brush it out. She brought out my fatherly side. I wouldn't violate my beliefs for her, but that didn't make me sexually repressed. Whenever appropriate, I intended to remind her of my proposal.

She didn't make it easy. Fly kept saying she was the bravest man he knew. The comparisons to a man were most appropriate. She had the morality of a typical modern man. My problem. Her problem.

"Albert," she said huskily, "have you reconsidered my offer?"

"Arlene, have you reconsidered my proposal?"

She started to respond but left her mouth open in mid-response. She looked cute that way. Then she got the words out: "You used the *p*-word."

"Sure did."

"Who would marry us?"

"Captain Hidalgo is the captain of our 'ship.' The medbot says he's recovering."

"I can just imagine how he'd react if we asked him to tie the knot."

I disagreed. "The captain has grown a lot on this mission. He's a better man. His horizons have expanded."

"Be hard not to change out here," she joked. I didn't laugh. There were times to be serious and this was one of them. "Arlene, will you marry me?"

I could tell she was disappointed in me. We were playing a game where I wasn't supposed to be so direct. It was okay for her to suggest any number of lewd acts, and that was acceptable. There was one rule, actually: I wasn't supposed to use the *p*-word.

She wasn't Fly's tough guy this time, not when she used my least favorite line of modern women: "It wouldn't be fair to you." I don't think there has been a woman since time began who believed that particular sentiment.

"I don't believe in fair. I believe in promises. You're

191

a woman of your word. You honor your commitments. We both know that. You're afraid to make a commitment you doubt you can keep."

"Then why do you keep asking me?"

I shrugged. "We belong together. I feel it in my bones."

She sighed. "We can't plan for the future."

I took her by the hand, and she made a fist over the ring. "Arlene, marriage isn't about planning for the future. It's a promise that can last five minutes or fifty years. Be honest. You're not afraid we won't have enough time together. You're afraid we'll have too much."

She pulled away so quickly the necklace dangling from her fist got caught on my thumb. It looked as if we were attached by an umbilical cord . . . and then we were separated.

She sounded like a little girl when she said, "I love you, Albert, but don't ever tell me how I feel. Or what I'm afraid of."

We'd faced the worst demons together. We'd sprayed death and destruction among the uglies from the deep beyond. But the gulf between us was deeper and darker and scarier than a steam demon's rear end.

This time we were rescued by Sarge—good old Flynn Taggart. He was back from his latest S&R session.

He was cheerful, at least. "If this keeps up, I'm trying out for a new career as translator to the stars. Captain Hidalgo will be with us in time for dinner. Sears and Roebuck have laid out the plan to me."

"Shouldn't they have waited until dinnertime for our briefing?" I asked.

He shook his head. "Not these guys, Albert. They figure what they say to one of us goes for all. I don't believe there are any ranks among the Klave."

We waited for Arlene to say something. We'd gotten in the habit. I must have upset her more than I realized. She didn't contribute. So I asked, "Do you think the captain will want us to be good marines when he's restored to us?"

I didn't mean to sound sarcastic. I had nothing against the captain. Arlene could vouch for that . . . when she wasn't pissed with me. But Fly took it as sarcasm.

"His call, mister! The captain is in command."

"Yes," Arlene finally spoke up. "Hidalgo is responsible for accomplishing the mission. We must do our best to support him."

Fly and she exchanged looks. There was a bond between them that nothing could ever weaken, including marriage.

"What did you learn from Sears and Roebuck?" she asked.

Fly told us.

We would accompany S&R on a little junket to the Fred base. The mission objective was some kind of super science weapon capable of initiating a resonant feedback that would wipe out all the computer systems of the bad guys.

Sounded good to me, but there was a hitch. The enemy base was twenty light-years away, and it had been hammered into all of us that *Star Trek* was wishful thinking. There were only slow boats to China.

The journey would take twenty years! Then it would take another twenty years for the feedback virus to be transmitted to all the Fred computers. The virus could only be installed on the system at the base. I wished we had Jill with us.

I had earned passing grades in school. I'd made change when I worked a cash register for my first real job. I could add numbers. *Forty years!*

"We'll spend the rest of our lives on this mission," I blurted out.

"No," said Fly cheerfully. "That's what I thought, too. It's not going to be that bad. We may not have FTL, but we do have access to ships that travel fast enough for our purposes. The trip will only be a few weeks of subjective time, even though it will count as forty Earth-years."

"What will Jill look like by the time we get back?" wondered Arlene.

We took a moment to mull that one over. Then Fly resumed his presentation on how to save the universe in one simple lesson. The plan sounded a lot more feasible than some of the other things we'd done.

We would leave the ship in orbit around a moon outside the Fred detection zone. On that moon was an experimental teleportation device based on Gate technology. We could use the experimental teleporter—theoretically, and by the grace of God—to reach the Fred base without the need of a receiver pad on the other end. As we'd discovered on Phobos, teleporters let you keep your gear. The plan ought to work.

As it turned out, the message aliens, the hyperrealists, had first discovered the Gates some three hundred thousand years ago and had been doing improvements ever since. Yes, discovered. No one knew who originally invented the Gates. The estimates for the oldest ones were the kind of numbers that give me a headache. There was an astronomer on TV who used to talk about "billions and billions" of years.

So what if this mode of travel had a few bugs in it? So did the American transportation system—the best the Earth had ever known.

I threw out a question: "Did you find out how the Freds took our guys by surprise? That's been troubling me ever since Sears and Roebuck started giving out with the history lessons."

Fly picked up a red ball from his unfinished meal off the floating table. I couldn't stand the taste of those things and hoped they'd come up with something better real soon now.

All of a sudden he had a devilish expression. "I wonder if I could throw this all the way up to the zero-g zone you used to coast in, Albert."

"Probably, but it wouldn't be polite."

Arlene agreed with me. "Don't do that, Fly."

"Well, they must have a remarkable garbage-disposal system," he said, "but I haven't see it work yet."

"Let's not find out it consists of enslaved marines," Arlene suggested wisely. I was glad to see her sense of humor returning.

"Point made," he said, popping the sphere into his mouth, and making a face before he swallowed. "I should've pitched it. Let me answer Albert. These aliens have a very interesting idea of a surprise attack. I wouldn't want to hire any of them as taxi drivers. Takes too long to get a cab now. They take forever to change anything! Once they achieved civilization it took millions of years for them to make the same amount of progress we did in—I don't know—say, ten thousand years?"

Arlene whistled. "Slow learners."

"Yeah," Fly continued. "Which is one reason the Fred attack took them by surprise. Sears and Roebuck say the attack came a lot sooner than expected—only thirty thousand years after the good guys established their observation base."

"Just like yesterday," I threw in. "So tell me, Fly, do you know what sort of opposition we may expect on our new mission?"

"Yes, Albert. After describing to Sears and Roebuck some of our adventures, like how we took down the spider-mind on the train, they said one thing."

"We're all ears," hinted Arlene, doing herself an injustice.

"They said, 'You ain't seen nothing yet!'"

26

I opened my eyes to a terrifying sight. A pulsing pole loomed over me, its mad eye blinking. There was a whirring sound, and I tasted copper in my mouth. And then something darted on the edge of my peripheral vision. It seemed to be circling, waiting to pounce.

Then the pole-thing moved out of the way so the flying thing could attack! I tried to move, but my limbs were immobile. I tried to shout for help but my throat was frozen. Right before the airborne object smashed into my face, I saw . . . a face on a blue ball.

A friendly face. A blue sphere. It was another of the blue spheres that had saved my life before. Now it was happening again. If this kept up, I'd think about taking some vitamins. I wasn't used to being an invalid.

The blue engulfed me, and I felt like a million bucks again. Then I could move all I wanted. I sat up and saw Corporal Arlene Sanders.

"Welcome back," she said.

"Do you mind if I put on some clothes?"

"No, sir," she said. Was that a smile pulling at the corners of her mouth? I was definitely alive.

The team looked one hundred percent. Whatever Taggart, Sanders, and Gallatin had been doing while I was laid up must have been good for them. They had so many things to tell me that formality would simply have gotten in the way. We were so far outside normal mission parameters that I realized the old adage of Gordon Dickson fully applied: "Adapt or die." The challenge was simply to keep Fly, Arlene, and Albert from interrupting each other as they took turns filling me in on the state of the mission as we ate our chow.

Mother of Mary! What had we gotten ourselves into? I wondered how many incredible things I was supposed to swallow along with the red things that tasted like very old tomatoes preserved in vinegar. Fly assured me they'd promised new and improved food soon. Arlene and Albert seconded the motion. If a sergeant and two corporals believed that strongly in something, I was going to eat all the little red things I could right now.

Seriously, I was pleased and impressed by what they had done while I was subject to the tender ministrations of what Arlene called the medical robot. Waking up to see something like that was not an experience to recommend.

No sooner had I gotten used to the medbot than along came Sears and Roebuck. I was glad they were on our side. I wouldn't want to blow away anything that looked the way they did.

"We are glad your unit is complete," they told us. I'd never had more unusual dinner companions. They ate little pyramids made out of some gelatinous substance. The pyramids were the exact same color blue as the spheres that kept saving my life.

Arlene warned me not to eat any food that wasn't human-approved. She needn't have worried. Being fire team leader didn't mean I had to commit suicide. I wanted to hang around for the mission with our new alien allies.

The medbot wouldn't leave my side until it was convinced my recovery was complete. While we munched, it volunteered some information. "For samples of Homo sapiens, all of you are recommended for upcoming missions of a military nature."

"We should hope so," I said.

"You are dopamine types."

"Huh?"

"It is a neurotransmitter strongly linked to seeking out adventure. You have many exon repetitions of the dopamine receptor gene. The genetic link to the D4 receptor. . . ."

"Wait a minute," interjected Albert. "Are you saying we are chemically programmed to want to kick demonic butt?"

"Yes," said the medbot.

Arlene clapped her hands. "This isn't one of those

pussy robots that says things like 'It does not compute.' This one's got English down."

"And without even going to college," sneered Fly.

"That's a cheap shot," Arlene threw back.

"Why do you do that?" asked the medbot.

"Do what?" asked Arlene.

"Call me a robot. I'm not a toaster. I'm not a VCR. I'm not a ship's guidance computer."

Arlene raised an eyebrow and asked, "What are you, then?"

"Organic tissues. Carbon-based life, the same as you."

"What's your name?" I asked the barber pole. Its answer did not translate into English. I tried my hand at diplomacy. "Would you mind if we continued calling you, uh, medbot?"

"No. That's a fine name. Please don't call me a robot."

Sears and Roebuck got us back on track. "Your unit and our unit are ready soon go to war." Their English might need work, but the meaning was clear. We shouldn't quarrel among ourselves, even if we were the type to seek out thrills and variety.

Sears and Roebuck looked at each other. They sure as hell appeared to be one character looking himself over in the mirror. They reached some kind of a decision and left the table, saying, "We are going to elsewhere. We are returning to here."

While they were absent, an alien who could have passed for a dolphin on roller skates with one arm snaking out of its head scooted over with another course of the dinner. This stuff looked almost like Earth food. It could have been enchiladas.

"Who is going to try this first?" I asked.

"Rank has its privileges," said Fly, the wise guy.

A Mexican standoff. Arlene played hero and took the first bite. I wish we'd had a camera to take her picture. "That's horrible," she said, doing things with her face that could have made her pass for one of the aliens.

"I'll try it," said Albert, proving there really was love between these two. It's not like they could keep it a secret. He proved himself a credit to his faith. His face didn't change at all, but the words sounded as if they were being pushed through a very fine strainer: "That is awful, but familiar somehow."

"Yes," Arlene agreed. "I can almost place it."

"This is not what I had in mind," Fly complained before he even tried it. "The mess was supposed to improve."

"It is a mess," agreed Arlene.

While Fly worked up his nerve, I tried the food. It sure as hell didn't taste like an enchilada, but I recognized the flavor right away. "*Caramba!* No wonder you recognize the flavor. It's choline chloride." The worst-tasting stuff this side of hell.

"Oh, no," said Fly, who had passed up eating the red balls while he waited for the "good stuff."

We'd all had to take choline chloride as a nutritional supplement. It was part of light drop training. The others remembered it from then. I was still using it, or had been right up to departure. The stuff was used by bodybuilders; it was as good for muscle tone as it was bad for the taste buds.

"I wonder what's for dessert," Fly said hopefully. Sears and Roebuck returned with the final course. But it wasn't something to eat.

"We have bringing you space suits for your unit," they said.

"Why have you brought us suits?" I asked, unable to recognize anything like space gear. They were carrying one thin box that would've been perfect for delivering a king-size pizza with everything on it.

"So you are going to your new spaceship," they announced. I wondered what I'd think of an alien craft. I already missed that old tub, the *Bova*.

"Where are the suits?" asked Arlene.

One of them opened the box. The other pulled out what appeared to be large sheets of Saran Wrap. And all I could think was: I should've stayed in bed.

I never thought I'd say this about an officer, but I was glad Hidalgo was with us again. He'd started out a typical martinet butthead. Now he insisted on being a human being. I guess if you drop an officer into a world of aliens and weird creatures, he has no choice but to turn human. The base must have been affecting me as well: Fly Taggart, the officer's pal!

Ever since we'd traveled over the rainbow I'd stopped worrying about Arlene's attitude toward Hidalgo. I'd worried what I would do if the guy turned out to be another Weems. Despite my complaining, I didn't think I could just stand by and let Arlene space a fellow marine. Didn't seem right somehow, even to an officer. I wasn't sure the end of civilization as we knew it meant open season on fragging officers. Anyway, it was ancient history now. We were a team in every sense of the word.

When S&R presented us with the high-tech space suits, it was a test for Hidalgo's command abilities. He'd been laid up for most of the tour of wonders, but he knew we weren't crazy when we briefed him.

All of us had a moment of thinking S&R were playing a joke on us. Hidalgo was in command. He had to decide that we were going all the way with our alien buds. We'd moved into a realm where ignorance could be fatal. The captain made the decision that counted, the same one we'd reached in our hearts and minds. Albert had the right word: "faith." We put our faith in the twin Magilla Gorillas.

Of course, we could rationalize anything. It wasn't until we were outside the base that I really believed the suits worked. We zipped up the damned things like sandwich bags that I prayed wouldn't turn into body bags.

Inside the airlock, we felt ridiculous. The transparent material draped around us like bad Halloween costumes. Only two parts of the suit were distinguishable from the Saran Wrap. The helmet was like a hood, hanging off the whole body of the material. The belt was like a solid piece of plastic. And that was it!

"Where's the air supply?" asked Arlene. S&R said it was in the belt.

"Where are the retros for getting around?" I asked. Same answer.

"How about communicators?" Hidalgo wanted to know. Ditto. And ditto.

Only one question merited a different response. "How tough is this material?" asked Albert.

"Can be damaged," said S&R. Nothing wrong with that sentence. Just the chilling reminder that however advanced these suits were, they didn't eliminate risk.

Once we were outside, the suits puffed up. We were comfortably cool inside them. Light was no problem, even though the sun was only a bright star at this distance. The base gave us all the light we needed. If we'd been in an orbit closer to home, we could have looked directly at old Sol and our eyes wouldn't have been fried. We were protected from all cosmic radiation. Hell, I wished PO2 Jennifer Steven could have one of these in her locker.

The first thing I noticed was a familiar constellation. Sure, the constellations were in slightly different locations in the sky. My sky. Fly sky. If there were picture windows in the base I would have figured out that we weren't as far from home as I thought.

The second thing I noticed was the ship S&R had promised us. It was right next to the base, and it was a big mother. The light from the base outlined it clearly, like a spotlight. We could make out all sorts of details. There were black shadows crisscrossing the ice.

Yeah, the ice. S&R had briefed us on all kinds of interesting details, such as the craft having an ion drive, the engine taking up most of the space. They'd neglected to mention that the entire ship was encased in a gigantic block of ice. The little voice in the back of my head made me promise to ask why when we returned to base, unless someone beat me to the $64,000 question.

S&R were carrying a small object with a box on one end and a tube on the other. They'd told us the little whatsit was actually a fusion-pumped laser torch. The rest of us carried nothing at all, so whatever could be done fell squarely on the shoulders of the dynamic duo. They reached the ice cube first and turned on their powerful toy.

We were busy mastering the use of the suits. It was hard to believe how much compressed gas was in those belts. When I snapped my right arm straight forward—in the same motion I would have used to knife somebody—the wrap became hard around the forearm. By twisting my hand I could activate the retros. Arm forward, suit forward. Arm back, suit back. Neat!

Albert was the first of us to master the suit. Go, marine! So he boosted himself over to help S&R. Arlene was next to get the hang of it well enough to join in. I had the idea that S&R didn't need any help. We were all along for the ride, to see the operation, and to become used to a higher-quality space suit.

We could hear each other's voices as clearly as if we were back in the "cafeteria." Hidalgo said a word or two, but he wasn't trying to tell S&R their business. I didn't see any need to horn in. I hung back, taking the watch, in case a space monster showed up or something.

When I heard the popping sound, I didn't realize it was inside Albert's helmet. I heard Arlene scream his name before I realized what had happened. There was debris making it hard to see. Then I pieced it together: Albert had been hit by the laser.

27

"Albert!"

I couldn't believe it as I reached out to him. He called my name faintly inside his hood: "Arlene, Arlene . . ."

The alien suits were so advanced that they seemed

like magic. But here was a grim reminder there was nothing supernatural about them. While S&R used the fusion-pumped laser torch, a high pressure bubble had ruptured. The explosion had compromised Albert's suit. I'd started to think the material couldn't be torn. Then, adding injury to injury, he was burned by the laser.

Sears and Roebuck switched off the torch as I held on to Albert. I saw him grimace through the hood and heard his choking gasp. Flecks of blood appeared on his face. I couldn't tell if the blood was coming up from his waist injury or if he was bleeding from his head. As he gasped, trying to catch his breath, I saw blood trickle from his gums. His face turned white.

"Get that man inside!" Hidalgo ordered.

S&R didn't move as I grabbed Albert, doing my best to ignore his groans. Suddenly Fly was beside me, helping me. I could hear Hidalgo's voice, talking to the aliens.

"They've got him," he said. "You can resume the operation." S&R were as silent as the depths of space. I couldn't bother with that now. My hands were full. In a situation like this, the most dangerous thing any of us could do would be to panic. Fly kept repeating, "Take it easy," but he didn't need to. I willed myself to move slowly and carefully. We were still getting the hang of the suits. There might be features that would surprise us . . . and spell Albert's death while we spun around trying to figure out which way was up.

We coasted toward the open lock as if we had all the time in the universe. The lock was a port in the storm. Momentum could be a monster or a friend, so we didn't hurry, despite the irrational child deep inside me demanding instant gratification.

Floating to the hospital. First aid for a brave marine. We wouldn't let Albert die. Wonder what they do with corpses in the alien base? Do they jettison them? Do they recycle them?

No! I wouldn't let myself think that way. Albert had helped mow down zombies, smash spider-minds, blow away steam demons, kick bony butt, and eat pumpkin pie. No freakin' way was it going to end now.

All we had to do was race against time and pay attention to the laws of physics. We didn't have to run and duck, fire and fall back, or even take turns on watch. We simply had to fall through the quiet gulfs of eternity, sailing between the stars, aiming not at a barrel of poison sludge but at a black dot that grew in size until it became the open hatchway only a few feet away.

Piece of cake.

We cycled through the lock. I was so worried about Albert that I barely noticed that his suit had already repaired itself. Unfortunately, the regenerative powers of the Plastic Wrap did not transfer to human tissue.

"The blue spheres," said Fly as we stripped off our hoods.

"Yes! Oh, my God, you're brilliant. We've got to contact the medbot right away." In another minute I'd be babbling.

We humped back to the main section of the base as we carried Albert between us. We'd left his suit on. It might not be a cure-all but as it resealed itself it helped stop the bleeding.

Medbot found us!

Its voice had always been pleasant. Now it was

music to my ears: "Sears and Roebuck sent a message. Part of your unit has been damaged."

I slowed down, caught my breath, tried to be coherent. "We need your help. We need one of those, oh, you know—the blue spheres that help sick people."

"They are called soul spheres."

"How . . . appropriate," whispered Albert, hanging on the edge of consciousness.

"Yes," Fly got into the act. "Like the one you used on Hidalgo."

The medbot's voice was unemotional but not a monotone. It could have been my imagination, but I thought it sounded sorry when it said, "That was the last one."

"What?" I asked, knowing full well what I'd just heard.

"This base is stripped down," it said. "We have all the necessities, but we are operating with a minimum of supplies."

All this time I thought we'd been in a transgalactic Hilton. This was their idea of roughing it? Maybe that was why we were having to thaw a spaceship out of a block of ice.

"This part of your unit will live," said the medbot. More music to my ears. "He will require a longer recovery time without a soul sphere."

I was afraid to ask how long. While I pondered the question, the medbot started to take him away.

"Wait!" Albert called out weakly. "I have to tell them something."

"Whatever you have to say will wait, big guy," said Fly. "You just get on the mend."

"No, I've got to tell you this," said Albert, his voice

growing stronger. "It'll save you valuable time dealing with Sears and Roebuck. Should have mentioned it to you earlier but the situation hadn't changed yet."

"Later," said Fly as the medbot began carting my Albert away.

He told the medico to hold up a minute. He hit us with: "Hidalgo can talk to them while it's just them, the same as you did, Fly. But I found out something when I had them synthesize the ring for Arlene, because we interacted with other aliens on the base. There's a trick to getting along with Sears and Roebuck. They think we're a group entity."

"I'd suspected the collectivism might go that deep," I admitted.

"Not collectivism," said Albert. "They're part of a true collective. A completely different thing! They can only understand group entities formed from powers of two—pairings of individual entities. They really can't understand *three* people operating as a unit."

So that was why Albert brought the holopicture of himself when he joined our session with S&R! But surely they must have realized it was some kind of virtual reality trick. Or maybe S&R just perversely refused to deal with unacceptable combinations. A cultural thing.

"You require medical attention," said the medbot. It sounded testy. Considering the absence of blue spheres, we weren't going to hold up Albert's surgery any longer. The barber pole hurried away, pulling Albert along on a pad.

"So here you are," said Captain Hidalgo, coming over to us. He was accompanied by S&R. "I hope Corporal Gallatin recovers," he said, watching the receding forms. "They did miracles with me, so I'm sure he'll be all right."

This seemed like a good time to test Albert's theory. Fly, that old mind reader, started the ball rolling: "Sears and Roebuck, would you mind telling us why your ship is encased in ice?"

S&R became agitated. They did the looking-at-each-other bit, but they started shaking their heads. They weren't in unison with each other.

Finally they tried communicating with the three of us. "Fly and Arlene, the ship was put into icing as part of ice comet going from cometary halo so avoiding detection." Then they started all over. "Fly and Esteban, the ship was put into icing as part of ice comet going from cometary halo so avoiding detection." Then: "Arlene and Esteban, the ship was—"

"Thanks, that'll do," said Fly. "We'll tell the others."

Captain Hidalgo had the aspect of a man whose brain had been sent out to the cleaners and had received too much starch.

Arlene took it like a man. She should have been happy. Captain Hidalgo had made an intelligent command decision. I would have to be left behind. I'd live. I'd be fine in several months, by Earth standard time. The mission couldn't afford to wait for my recovery. Hidalgo had needed only a few days to heal. He was the CO. I was baggage.

And while I grew old, Arlene would stay young. Maybe that was as it should be. For all her guts and strength, she made me think of a vulnerable child. I'd always wanted to be a patriarch, and now it looked as if I'd at least look like one by the time I saw her again. If I saw her again.

I could have predicted it before she said it: "You're the man I want to marry. You're my man."

I believed the latter. I had faith that she believed the former, so long as they were only words. As she stood by my bed and we held hands, I performed the simple calculation in my head. I'd be sixty-seven years old when she returned.

"I love you, Arlene."

"That's not what I want to hear you say."

I squeezed her hand and told her, "I know you really love me, Arlene. That doesn't change what you are—a helluva marine who will do her duty, no matter what."

The others were waiting to say their farewells. "Call them in," I said.

"No. Not until we've settled something."

Probably just as well that we weren't planning nuptials. This woman wasn't obedient. She crawled right on the bed with me. I guess you could call it a bed, even though it was a lot better than most. Sort of an overbed or superbed.

"Arlene?" I tried to get her attention. "Just because I'm laid up doesn't mean the rules have changed."

"What was that about 'laid'?" she asked, smiling wickedly.

"Arlene."

"Albert."

"You're not going to ask to make love again, are you?"

"You will make love only to your wife," she breathed into my ear.

"That's right."

"All right."

I'd been through so much lately that I no longer

trusted my hearing. My eardrums still ached from my adventure outdoors. "Arlene, what did you just say?"

"I said yes, you big dope. I'm accepting your proposal of marriage."

I wanted to shout yippee and dance a jig. Couldn't do that, so I settled for crushing her in my arms and kissing her. This was no brother-sister kiss.

While we caught our breath, my brain started firing on all cylinders again. "But what about the mission?" I asked.

She put her head on my chest, and I ran my hand over her red carpet. Then she lifted up her face and drilled me with the most beautiful emerald-green eyes in the galaxy. "I'm still going," she said. "But we'll have time for the honeymoon."

"How long?" I dared ask.

"Six days," she said softly. "Captain Hidalgo says we'll have six days. We can count on it. He'll be marrying us."

I kissed her again.

"You won't wear the silly G-string and pasties, will you?" I asked.

"How could I? That stuff's back on the *Bova.*" She nibbled my ear.

"But Sears and Roebuck can synthesize anything," I protested.

Her lips fluttered over my eyelids and came to rest on my left cheek. "They can't synthesize everything." Her voice was muffled against my skin.

"Well, I would sort of like you . . . natural, you know," I confessed, emphasizing my point by licking her all-natural neck.

"I'll be the girl next door," my wife-to-be promised.

"Need I ask if you've picked a best man?"

We both laughed. It's not as if we'd give Fly Taggart any choice. I considered the merits of asking Sears and Roebuck to whip up a tuxedo for the ultimate marine. There was something about S&R's name that inspired the idea.

28

Dear Albert,

If I write this letter quickly enough you may receive it before too many years elapse. Sears and Roebuck gave me the idea. The same technology that makes Gate travel possible, not to mention this incredible spaceship, allows me to use the sub-light post office. The laser messages don't move much faster than the ship at max, but remember how fast the ship is moving! If we'd been crazy enough to send a message ahead of us to the Fred base so they could roll out the red carpet, we would have arrived about a half hour after they received the message.

"Sub-light" is a term that doesn't do these speeds justice. Traveling an inch an hour is under the speed of light. Both the Freds and our guys can travel right up to that speed. S&R's ship will reach a maximum speed of 99.99967 miles per hour, relative to the Earth. Isn't that incredible? Gate travel without the Gate.

I wish you could have seen the ship from the outside when we finished melting off the ice. I swear it looked just like a cigar. Fly didn't pick up on my reference to Frank R. Paul, the science-fiction artist from the 1930s who created a lot of stogie spaceships. That style went out of fashion in the 1950s when the flying-saucer craze started.

I suppose there are only so many shapes and forms possible. The human race has expended so much energy trying to conceive of every possibility that we couldn't help but get a few things right. By the way, I meant to say this to you before, so I better do it now: I do believe there is every bit as much imagination and intelligence in religion as there is in science fiction. There'd have to be. It's just that what you take as revelation I assume to be imagination.

Before the demons came, I thought the universe was pretty dull and predictable. It only took seeing my first zombie on Phobos to change my mind about that. Forever.

Like this ship, for instance. I love it. Poor Fly hates it. He can't stop bitching. I don't mean complaining. I don't mean kvetching. I mean bitching.

He was spoiled by the artificial gravity on the base. I sort of regretted leaving the *Bova*. Zero-g is great for my tits. I forgot you don't like that word. Breasts, I mean. When it comes to outer space, the female body is simply better designed than the male. Why do you think God did that to you poor guys? Sorry, you know I'm only kidding.

Oh, I told you Fly was complaining, and then I

went off on a tangent without telling you his problem. The Klave ship is a zero-g baby, just like the *Bova*. If feet could talk, mine would whimper for joy. I could spend my life in free fall. You know how I feel about that after our honeymoon. I'm so glad we found that sealed compartment in one of the zero-g areas. You needed to keep off your feet, darling.

When Fly found out he'd be living in zero-g again, his first words were "Oh, man!" You know how irritated he becomes. Even so, Hidalgo convinced him that the ship is brilliantly designed. It's two kilometers long. Well, you already know that. We could see this was no dinghy when it was in the ice. It has a central corridor connecting all the engine pods. There are no real compartments. Sears and Roebuck don't believe in privacy. The Klave would be Ayn Rand's nightmare.

Anyway, there is no provision for spinning or any other artificial gravity. There is a very good reason for this. S&R told us there can be no gravity generators on their ship like the ones they have on the base. It's flat-out impossible. The gravity maker where you are makes use of existing properties of matter. They say it's impossible for a ship accelerating to near light-speed to use one of these devices. Mass increases, you know, as far as physical measurements are concerned in our local area. The Klave ship is increasing sufficient gravity on its own. In other words, if they used the gravity generator, it would be impossible to accelerate to the necessary speed. So thanks to these laws of physics, my feet and breasts win while Fly's stomach loses.

Don't I write wonderful love letters, darling?

Would you enjoy hearing some more technical stuff? Or would you rather devour every word of my wildest fantasy? Well, I don't want to add to your frustration. So I'll tell you more about the Fly ride.

The chairs—yes, we have chairs—can be put in any position within the ship. They will be on the ceiling when we decelerate. Fly keeps saying they're not as comfortable as what we had on the base. You see, I wasn't kidding about our big tough marine being spoiled.

S&R are proud of their ship. Until now I didn't realize they were capable of pride. Unless I'm losing my mind, they are easier to understand when they are bragging about the ship. I may be imagining their pride, but I'd make book that the Klave have no concept of sentimentality, any more than they do of privacy. The Klave do not give ships names. I suggested they call this one the *Kropotkin*, after my favorite collectivist, a left-wing communitarian anarchist.

A quick aside: did you know that S&R come from a planet with a heavier gravity than Earth? Imagine the backaches they must have under 1.5 gravity. No wonder they like a zero-g ship.

Back to the subject of the ship, here are a few more specs. It takes three to four Earth-standard days for us to accelerate to the max, then three to four more days to bring this sucker to a full stop. When S&R said the ship moves relativistically, I asked if the Klave were more like cousins or brothers and sisters. They didn't get the joke, but Hidalgo howled with laughter.

We've learned a lot of things that would interest you, beloved. First, here's something had been bothering Fly all along. Why did the Freds attack Earth in the first place? What was their motivation? The most they can extract from human survivors is slave labor, and slaves are expensive to maintain; it's more economical to use machines.

Fly and the captain and I wrestled over these problems before we laid them out to Sears and Roebuck. There are no natural resources that can't be obtained elsewhere, and more easily, I would think. S&R told us how their side figured out that the Freds were eventually going after Earth. They did this by analyzing the Fred pattern of play up until that point. Of course, such an analysis wouldn't indicate why the Earth was chosen as a target in the first place.

During the tens of thousands of years when the good guys were in orbit around the Earth, watching and observing, they did their best to comprehend the attraction of what Fly calls the old mud ball.

Hidalgo suggested there might have been a Fred observatory on Earth for even longer. For this insight, S&R pronounced us a most logical unit. That turns out to be why the hyperrealists only risked a small base and a single star-drive ship, the one that brought them to Earth.

S&R admits that there is something strange about us humans, other than the problem of dealing with us in odd-number combinations. I never thought of S&R as understanding subtlety, because that seems to go with the concept of privacy, but they hinted there is something very strange about human beings. Apparently this amazing discovery fit right into the plans of the Freds. S&R didn't want to tell us what it is!

We played a trick on Captain S&R. Once we'd convinced ourselves that the ship was safely on automatic pilot, Hidalgo, Fly, and I surrounded the spearmint twins in a triangle and began firing rapid questions. The questions didn't really matter. Fly asked who won the World Series. Hidalgo wanted to know if the Soviet Union would have toppled without a nudge from Ronald Reagan. I wanted to know what the outcome would be of a fight between one spider-mind and ten pumpkins.

S&R couldn't figure out who the hell was talking to them. They were so totally freaked at being assaulted by three entities at a time that it wouldn't have surprised me if they'd left the ship! Let's face it, Albert, we were torturing our new friends. But it's not as if we had any choice. We had to have that information.

With all of us talking at once, S&R couldn't figure out the proper pairings of two. It must have been like finding themselves in the middle of an Escherian geometrical figure that cannot exist in the real world, or in this universe, anyway. S&R collapsed as if we'd let the air out of them and they'd decompressed.

Fly and Hidalgo started a swearing contest. If we'd killed them, we'd buggered the mission and any hope for Earth. Fortunately, all we'd done was give them a splitting headache—like in the old TV commercials where your head hurts so much it takes two of you to feel all the pain.

We got what we wanted—except maybe we didn't want it after all. When S&R recovered, they told us all they knew. Humans, it turns out, are different from every other intelligent species in the galaxy. You'll never believe what the difference is. Then again, maybe you will.

Humans die.

Hidalgo spoke for all of us when he asked, "So what? Who doesn't?"

We didn't want to hear the answer about all intelligent life forms except us. I've never been an egalitarian, but the news didn't seem fair.

When a member of an intelligent species other than Homo saps is damaged beyond repair, the body becomes totally incapacitated, the same as us, but it doesn't end there. The individual (and here we may even refer to S&R as individuals) is still conscious. If the body is totally destroyed, that consciousness remains. We would call it a ghost.

These ghost-spirits are easily and consistently detected. They commonly jump into new bodies as they're being born—on those rare occasions when there is a birth. As soon as the physical components mature sufficiently to allow communication, they indicate who they were in the previous incarnation. Then they can pick up where they left off.

When I learned this, I naturally thought of our many arguments in the time we've known each other. Maybe we aren't as far apart as we think. My materialism has run into a brick wall of the spirit. Your general faith may be stronger with this knowledge, but the details must disturb any-

one with orthodox convictions. I never did ask
you if you were bothered by the nearest English
translation of the name of the life-saving entities:
"*soul* spheres."

Even though S&R weren't deliberately holding
anything back from us, it was difficult to piece
together everything I'm writing you. Sometimes
it seems as if they're starting to master our
language, but then out come the fractured sentences again.

The ghost-spirit-consciousness is freed only
when the body is *totally* annihilated. Naturally
Fly asked them what they meant by "totally."
Neither Hidalgo nor I desired to learn that particular fact. We were still reeling from the discovery
that our mortality was unique to humankind. Fly
acted as if he was in the market for an alien body
and wanted to check out the mileage.

S&R answered that total annihilation occurred
when less than eight percent of the original body
mass was chemically dispersed, but there were
different rules for different individuals. I'm not
sure how this applies in the case of the Klave
collective, but for other species they take an
especially useful specimen and destroy the body
before the final death rattle, thus freeing the
ghost-spirit to be reincarnated and to continue
working that much sooner.

You'd think that would be sufficient to conquer
death. But wait, there's more. S&R had described
the way the system worked, stretching back into
the dim mists of time. But science marches on,
even with slow evolvers. Techniques were developed to repair almost destroyed bodies. Dead

people could be revived in their original forms. In all sorts of ways, the aliens of our galaxy defeated death before we ever encountered our first doom demon.

Mortality simply didn't occur to them. Why should it have? They had all sorts of ways to deal with the limbo of endless waiting. They didn't need to deal with death. This was true of both the good guys and the bad guys. They collected their dead and arranged them in temples and theaters where they staged elaborate entertainments, debates, classes, lectures, and you-name-it to keep the "deceased" occupied. This was necessary because there are not enough births to accommodate the soul supply. So untold number of consciousnesses remain in a death trance until a body becomes available.

Albert, you were closer to these creatures in your certainty that consciousness goes on forever. My atheism is inadequate to describe their reality. But from our point of view, the human point of view, this seems a victory for me. I'm not happy about it. They say no one ever fully dies, except humans!

I can hear you answering me right now. I imagine your mouth pressed to my shoulder, forming the word that resolves all these problems for you: God. What will you say when I inform you that no other intelligent species in the galaxy has a belief in gods or God? Only we do, Albert. Only the human race.

At last I have a faith as deep as yours, beloved. We've made a contract together, and I intend to live by it. That's why you had such a struggle talking me into it. When I make a plan, or agree to someone else's, I stick to it. I don't change it on a whim. A contract is a sacred trust.

So I know what I believe in at last. It isn't religion. It isn't God. It's you, Albert dearest. You are the meaning of my life.

Your faithful Arlene

29

It was my fault. Good old Fly Taggart can't leave well enough alone. The mission was proceeding without a hitch. So what if I was pissed about being in zero-g again? Arlene was in her natural element. Hidalgo was doing all right. Only Yours Truly had a problem with it.

I was bored. We'd only been out from the base a couple of weeks, Earth standard time. We'd learned a hell of a lot about the galaxy in which the human race counted for one lousy enemy village. Talk about waking up and smelling the coffee. Finding out you're a member in good standing of the most ignorant "intelligent species" in the universe is depressing. At least it was to me.

So we were poured onto an alien spacecraft where we were about as useful as Girl Scouts at the Battle of the Bulge. While S&R upshipped us to Fred Land, there wasn't much for us to do except sit back and twiddle our thumbs.

I shouldn't squawk. Jeez, Arlene finally bedded down with the man of her dreams and then she ships out with the rest of us. My best buddy had a few quirks of her own, though. If she and Albert weren't going to be separated this way, I could imagine her putting off the moment of truth indefinitely. As it turned out, she never hesitated for a moment about following orders. Hidalgo had won her respect, but even if he hadn't, she would have come along for the good of the mission. I know Arlene Sanders.

I mean Arlene Gallatin. I'll never forget Albert ordering me to take care of her. So what else is new?

The stupidest thing a soldier can do is wish away the tedium. He may receive a face full of terror. Trouble with me is I've never been a soldier. I'm a warrior. Which means I don't relish long periods of enforced idleness, especially if I'm floating around like an olive in the devil's martini.

Sears and Roebuck tried to find work for us. Trouble was that the shipboard routine was more automated here than it was on the *Bova*. Of course, that's like saying there's less for an Apache warrior to do on an aircraft carrier than in a canoe. Aboard the *Bova*, the navy was in charge. Here the high technology was so high that no one needed to be in charge, except S&R. I don't know why I thought it could have been otherwise. Stupid human pride is not a monopoly of the Marine Corps, no matter what the pukeheads in the other services say.

There was one useful task. Someone had to prepare the program for insertion and figure out what we were going to do when we lifted the eight-week, forty-year siege and returned. One guess who was the least qualified member of the crew for that job! Not that I couldn't have stumbled through it. And my bud would have been the first to admit that Jill was more qualified than Hidalgo or her. (How I would have loved to pass that information on to my favorite teenager.)

I became so desperate that I hunted around for something to do. We had plenty of the special space suits but no need to go outside. I hinted to the captain that maybe one of us should take a look-see topside, but they saw right through me, as easy as looking through one of the suits. They did at least show me the weapons we'd be using at the Fred base. Ray guns! Honest-to-God ray guns. They required no maintenance whatsoever.

At least on the *Bova* there were books. I had found a copy of *The Camp of All Saints.* I didn't have a memory like Albert's, but I remembered the passage about how civilization is what you defend behind the gun, and that which is against civilization is in front of the gun. A good marine credo. I'd thought about that while we were on the hyperrealist base. It was strange having no weapons the entire time we were there. But nothing was attacking us. The subject never came up except with Albert, and he said, "There's no gun control where the mind is the only weapon."

When we first arrived at that base, Albert may have thought he'd entered heaven. Before we left, Arlene did her best to convince him he really had. I was going to miss Albert.

Arlene showed me a copy of the letter she lasered her man. She crammed an awful lot in there. She is endlessly fascinated by S&R and their ship. I'm still depressed. I wish faster-than-light were possible. Whether we succeed or fail in upcoming missions, I have the sinking feeling we'll never see our own civilization again. If that's how it comes down, then the Freds and their demonic hordes will have succeeded in ending my civilization for me.

"You've got to hand it to the Klave," said Captain Hidalgo. "The food is getting better."

He was right about that. The last batch of experimental food tasted almost like a passable TV dinner. Sort of a combination meat loaf and chocolate pudding. At least it was edible.

"Yeah, they're real pals," I said. Realizing how that sounded, I went on. "I'm not criticizing them. They're the only friends humanity has on this side of the ditch."

Arlene drifted into the conversation. "they were the official experts on humans. The other message aliens didn't have high enough security clearances to deal with us."

That was a revelation. "So the others weren't actually bored to death with us?"I asked, attempting not to sound too autobiographical.

"Well, maybe they were," said Arlene thoughtfully. "What matters is why Sears and Roebuck became so interested in Earth. They had no idea why we were so different from them. We were considered counterbiological because perpetual consciousness is considered essential to the definition of intelligent organisms used everywhere else in the galaxy."

Hidalgo shook his head in wonder. "If it bleeds, it

lives," he said. "The monsters must think we live just long enough to massacre us."

"Remember we're talking about how these advanced beings view sapience," said Arlene. "We consider ourselves biological because we define a biological system as one that works like ours."

"These guys have a definition we don't fit," I volunteered.

"Right," agreed Arlene. "Let's say they have a more universal definition. Just as they have expanded our horizons, we've done the same for them."

"So where do the monsters fit into this?" asked Captain Hidalgo. A damn good question. Seemed like a long time since we'd had to blow away any hellprinces, deep-fry an imp, or barbecue a fat, juicy spider-mind.

"I've thought about that a lot," said Arlene. "The Freds understand humanity better than the Klave and the other message aliens. I believe the Freds are afraid of humans. Their ultimate goal is not to enslave but to wipe out humanity."

"They've made a good start," muttered Hidalgo.

There was no arguing with that. Arlene did her best to lift our spirits, assuming we had any: "Sears and Roebuck are dedicated to saving us from the Freds. Their logic is sound. If we weren't a threat to the Freds they never would have launched a full-scale invasion."

I respected the way S&R thought. They didn't have a clue to what made us special, and neither did I. But we hadn't spent all this time swimming in sludge, muck, and blood to no purpose. We rated because we were hated.

That conversation was the high point of a whole

day. Earth. Standard. Time. Twenty-four hours. Lots and lots of minutes. Being ordered to relax is hard enough. It takes a real genius to do plenty of nothin'.

So, just like the rawest recruit, I wished something would happen to break the tedium. And something did. And I felt that it was all my fault. I didn't used to be superstitious. Or at least not very. But that was in the days before Phobos, before Deimos, before Salt Lake City and Los Angeles. Back when I thought Kefiristan was a problem.

Back when the universe made sense and I didn't believe in space monsters. I'm not talking about monsters that come from space. It was enough of a stretch to accept a leering red gnome stumbling through an alien Gate. However, some things should be impossible. Like the space monster that came out of nowhere—there was a lot of nowhere out here—and attacked the Klave ship.

At first I thought S&R were projecting an entertainment program. The three-dimensional object darting over our heads looked like a refugee from a Japanese monster movie. I'd never been into those when I was a kid, but when Arlene and I were going to movies together, she dragged me off to a whole day of Godzilla and Gamera movies sponsored by *Wonder* magazine. She'd picked up free tickets because she was a subscriber.

I didn't care for any of the films, but the images were too ridiculous to forget. Naturally I assumed— always a bad idea—that the thing on display, courtesy of S&R, was of the same kidney. It even looked like a kidney, but it had a shell, and several tentacles and heads stuck out of it at odd angles. At least it didn't have wings. Wings would've been *really* stupid.

"Bile nozzle!" screamed Sears and Roebuck. I didn't know they could scream. They were so freaked that their stubby little legs started a running motion, even though it made no difference in zero-g. I suddenly realized how fast these suckers could move at the bottom of a gravity well. Here their legs only looked funny, like hummingbirds' wings, as they became a blur. These guys were definitely upset.

"Bile nozzle?" echoed Arlene.

"Closest in English," they answered, more calmly now that they were past the initial shock. Their legs slowed down, too.

I didn't think I'd ever be bored again. Not only were S&R aware of this flying space organ, they had a name for it. Just like in those Japanese movies where the kids automatically know the name of every oversized sea urchin that has designs on Tokyo.

"The ship is attracting to bait," said S&R. "Inertial energy turns into heating."

God help me, I understood them perfectly. "From outside, this ship must look like a star," I said.

"Unless . . . until we decelerate," Hidalgo reminded himself as much as the rest of us.

"So that monster is chasing a small star," said Arlene. "What does it eat?"

"Anything," said S&R. "Not only carbon. Other chemistries! But only from the inside. We must go to away. We're already burning fuel now."

"There isn't any way we can fight this creature?" Hidalgo asked, his voice icy.

S&R had one of their periodic attacks of schizophrenia. One head nodded while the other shook. That didn't mean they intended the same meaning by those motions we did; but it sure fit the situation like a glove.

"No time for going to escape maneuvers," they said. "Bile nozzle already matching velocipedes."

"Velocities!" I shouted. I couldn't stop correcting these guys, but I understood the problem. This ship was not a Millennium Falcon we could use in a dogfight or a monster fight. The ship used inertial dampers to get rid of the incredible amounts of energy we were using. At 100,000 gravities acceleration, S&R didn't want to make a trivial error that would turn us all into smears of jelly.

All that I understood. Bile nozzle was beyond me. Just outside the ship. And whether we sped up or slowed down, that thing was going to stick to us like blood on a combat boot.

"How will it attack?" asked Hidalgo.

"Becomes one unit," said S&R. That could only mean the thing split into two. "Inside ship part."

"I've got an idea," said Arlene with an eagerness that meant she had a damned good one. "How soon will some part of this monster be inside the ship?"

"Going to now," said S&R worriedly.

She nodded, and I knew what the movement of *her* head meant! "Tell me, if we can hurt that part, how will the outside part respond?"

"Bile nozzle will go to elsewhere," said S&R. They sounded hopeful.

"Okay," said Arlene. I recognized her patented early-bird-that-got-the-worm smile.

"Out with it, marine," Hidalgo ordered, as hopeful as the rest of us.

Arlene said, "Bring me three space suits, every portable reactor pack in the ship, and the biggest goddam boot you can find!"

30

These were the best marines I'd ever served with. Corporal Taggart-Gallatin's plan was brilliant. I never would have thought of it. I doubted the aliens would have come up with it because they were so terrified of the thing they called a bile nozzle.

While we suited up, we could see the space entity right next to the ship. It was difficult to distinguish the heads from the tentacles—if those *were* heads . . . or tentacles. The new menace reminded me of the sea beast we'd encountered in the Pacific, I didn't see how either of these creatures could actually be alive. Their shapes shifted and changed when you tried to get a good look.

The largest of the bile nozzle's heads, which was right next to the ship, was a cloud of swirling colors in which one shape kept repeating itself: a crow's head, with a bright dot that bounced around where the eye ought to be. The damned head seemed to regard the ship like a tasty treat.

Sears and Roebuck insisted that the thing wasn't dangerous until part of it was inside the ship. Arlene's plan couldn't stop it from joining our little party, but she was one woman who could handle a gate-crasher.

S&R insisted on coming with us. They didn't act as if they were the captain and we were under their command. Cooperation was more natural to them than command. A few years ago I thought Earth was the only inhabited planet. Now that I'd had my eyes opened to new possibilities, I didn't expect everyone in the universe to follow my military code. Only a martinet butthead would expect that.

The marines could handle this assignment, but S&R were probably afraid to remain inside. I couldn't blame them, because right before we cycled through the airlock, some damned thing materialized only a few feet away.

"Hurry! Go to outside," urged S&R.

Fortunately the monster hadn't finished forming itself yet. When it became completely solid, we'd be the first items on its menu. According to S&R, the monster liked to start with carbon-based life forms as an appetizer. Then it would go to work on the ship itself.

Before we went outside, I had a good look at the face forming so close that I could have spit at it. Steam demons were handsome compared to it. Hell-princes would have been first choice for a blind date. The most hideous imp could have passed as Mr. America by comparison.

The eyes were the opposite of the glowing orb in the crow's head. All three were burning black dots, reminiscent of a fire eater's. They were attached to a tube ending in an orifice that was apparently both mouth and nose. Yellow liquid dribbled out of the tube and sizzled against the side of the ship. An acid that sounded exactly like frying bacon! All this happened while the head was blurring around the edges as it

struggled to complete itself. The thing made a snuf-
fling, snorting sound.

"Bile nozzle" seemed an apt name.

Arlene went first, kicking off from the bulkhead and
hurtling out through the hatch. We exited from the
starboard side of the ship. Seemed like a good idea,
because the remainder of the monster was on the port
side. We worked fast before the enemy could become
curious.

Every time I used one of these transparent space
suits I became a little less nervous about how flimsy
they appeared. If Corporal Gallatin had been wearing
one of the navy pressure suits when he had his
accident, his lungs would have ruptured in the vacu-
um. I was beginning to understand what Gallatin
meant about faith. I too had faith in this alien
technology.

We implemented Arlene's plan before the monster
got wise. Our extra-vehicular activity consisted of
attaching the portable reactor packs to the outside of
the ship. Then we turned them on and let them do the
work.

Slowly, oh, so very slowly, the packs began to turn
the ship. We hovered in space like a hung jury. We
were counting on one thing: that a creature which
spent its entire existence in a weightless condition
would have no familiarity with gravity. If our ship
had been spinning it would have left us alone.

If Arlene's theory proved correct, the bile nozzle
would experience something brand-new: the with-
drawal of an invitation. A subtle hint he should go
elsewhere. Or go *to* elsewhere, as S&R would have
said.

We were patched into the ship through our suits.
Before the monster realized there was a problem, it

made a kind of contented snoring sound. It didn't take much to get the creature's attention. The ship was spinning at 0.1 gravity when the snore changed to a howl of rage and desperation. Heavy thudding and liquid noises preceded its exiting the craft.

We didn't witness the part reuniting with the whole. We saw something better: the huge creature—maybe a third the length of the ship—zooming off into infinity. From this angle we could see what passed for its back—a series of tubes boosting the cloudlike swirling mess that was the rest of it. Right before it went out of range, the mass seemed to grow solid into something I'd compare to a turtle's shell. If I ever met Commander Taylor again I'd recommend this thing for membership in the Shellback Society.

I never did find out why Arlene wanted the biggest goddam boot we could find.

When we were safe aboard, there were new troubles. S&R's ship was not designed to take such acceleration along its radial axis. The structure had sustained severe damage and was leaking air like a son of a bitch. There were so many split seams we would never be able to patch them all.

"We have no plan for to use airless ship," said S&R, "but not to worry."

Not to worry? Where had I heard that before? Oh, it was from *Mad* magazine. Alfred E. Newman looked just like the last president of the United States. A fire eater had turned him into toast. It was worse than any congressional investigation.

"Why shouldn't we worry?" I wanted to know.

"Space suits," they answered.

"We've lost time dealing with this monster," observed Arlene. "There can't possibly be enough air in the suits for the remainder of the trip."

Both Arlene and Fly insisted that S&R had no sense of humor, but the sound that came out of the alien mouths sounded like laughter to me. "Not to worry," they repeated. "Enough air in belts for human life span!"

I wasn't the least bit surprised. We were ready to prove what tough guys we were. Marines! We could hold our breath longer than anyone, even those Navy SEALS on the *Bova*. We could hunker down in our suits as we slowly ran out of air . . . and not complain one time. Tough guys don't complain. We could take it. We'd die without complaint, because we weren't weaklings. We weren't some inferior form of life. We weren't civilians.

As I looked at Fly and Arlene—they'd be first names to me for the rest of my life—I wondered if they felt the way I did. I've never met a sane marine. I'm not sure there is such a breed. That's why my wife divorced me. Damned civilian.

Arlene shot off one of her clever remarks: "A sufficiently advanced technology greatly reduces the number of cliffhangers."

So we'd come to this: we were a charity case in the custody of superior beings. We could kid ourselves all we wanted, but we were not as good as the aliens who ruled the galaxy. It was our good fortune to become pets to one side in a galactic war. The other side saw us as a nuisance.

Fly spoke for all humanity when he demanded to know more about that other side. "No more surprises," he told S&R. "You should have warned us about creatures like that bile nozzle thing. Did the Freds send it?"

"Not coming from the Fred," they assured him.

"Just another creature who has received the Lord's

precious gift of life," Fly sneered. "Well, it doesn't matter, now that we've kicked its butt. Fill us in on the Freds. What are they like?"

S&R hadn't fought the Freds all this time without picking up a bit of knowledge. Our alien allies weren't idiots. I was the idiot for not having requested this information myself. I feared that I was beginning to lose it. When the devils first appeared on Phobos and Deimos, it was a surprise to Fox Company. There was no briefing for Fly and Arlene. There was only survival. Before my fire team set foot on Phobos, I had pumped our fearless heroes for everything they remembered about Phobos and Deimos. S&R were the duo to pump now.

The briefing consisted of projected images and a basic description of the main enemy, delivered in S&R's funny English. I gasped when I saw that a Fred head looked like an artichoke. Eyeballs were sprinkled over their domes like raisins in a cake. The heads seemed a little small to me, but there was a good reason for this: The brains weren't in the heads; the gray matter was housed in a safer place, down lower, in the armored chest. There was room there for a very large brain. The arms attached to the chest were rubbery affairs with semiarticulated chopsticks for fingers.

"Avoid them sticking into you," said S&R.

"The fingers?" I prompted. The image showed us just what those fingers could do. Contained in tough but flexible skin sacks, the chopsticks were hard and sharp. With a flick of its rubbery arms, a Fred could make any or all of its fingers opposable.

Moving on down the torso, we came to a waist so narrow I didn't see how it could support the weight it carried. Then there were two thick legs, each ending in a foot that was very like a human foot, except that it included one feature of a bird's claw: a toe in back, protruding from the otherwise human-looking foot.

I wondered what S&R's feet were like, but I wasn't curious enough to ask them to remove their boots.

Fly told us that the Freds wore tightly fitting boots. "Magnetized to them walking," said S&R. "They are not liking free-falling."

"How reasonable!" Fly blurted out, and then the reality hit him. "Shit. You mean their ships are zero-g too?"

"Same principles appliance," said S&R.

"The same principles apply." Arlene corrected them this time.

"Tell me something else," demanded an irritated Fly. I didn't stop the sergeant, because I agreed with him. "Were you going to let us fight the Freds without giving us any background?"

"Humans like going to be surprised," answered S&R.

"Maybe humans like going into situations blind," said Fly. "Military men have more brains than that."

And their brains are in the right place, I added mentally.

Then we reached the important subject: weapons. The Freds did not keep an armory on their ship equivalent to what even a self-respecting imp or zombie would pack. Basically they didn't expect to be attacked. Pride goeth before the fall.

Despite their confidence, every Fred carried a personal weapon that was fairly nasty. S&R warned us to keep an eye out for that. The weapons looked like slingshots with more moving parts and used an electromagnetic field to fire little flying saucers.

S&R summed up: "We have no plan for to fight past

making sabotage at Fred base. Other weapons they may be bringing to exteriorize."

"Do you mean exterminate?" asked Fly.

The briefing improved my morale. I threw out: "Whatever you mean, Captain Sears and Roebuck, rest assured the United States Marine Corps always has a plan to kick butt."

After the crash course in Freds 101, the remainder of the trip was nothing to write home about. It was like the first part of the trip. The only difference was that we were wrapped in cellophane so we'd be nice and fresh at the other end.

All good things come to an end.

All bad things come to an end.

"A teleporter ought to be nothing for you after your Gate problem," Arlene said, trying to cheer me up.

The damage to S&R's ship provided an unexpected tactical advantage. We might never return to the message alien base, but now we had a nice decoy to distract the Freds while we used the teleporter. S&R sent the remains of their ship straight at a Fred defense satellite. We hated to see it go. It was a good ship.

Disembarking from a ship had never been easier. There was no damage to the airlocks. We were already suited up and ready to go teleport-hunting. All in a day's work.

I would have said that if you've seen one transmatter device, you've seen them all, but that wasn't true. This one didn't have a stone arch built over it with lots of weird crap carved into it, though.

I might have used my experience with the Gate on Phobos as an excuse for being superstitious, but there was no point. Much of what we'd seen since leaving our solar system made no sense according to our physics. So there was nothing for us to do but have faith in the engineering that worked. None of the amazing alien technology had let me down yet, except for one small Gate glitch.

I waited my turn and took a deep breath. Then I stepped forward to meet my destiny.

31

I'd never heard a hairy bag of protoplasm call out my name before: "Fly!"

Looking down, I noticed something glistening on the floor near my boot. I was slow on the pickup because I had my priorities. First, the boot. That meant we still had our clothes and weapons. Second, we were back in gravity. So what if my back hurt and my arches complained? Gravity, sweet gravity. Third . . . third, there was some kind of problem.

Liquid was leaking from the flesh bag. It was sort of a faded pink I'd never associated with blood. I took a closer look at the bag and recognized a human mouth. I'd never seen a mouth all alone before, surrounded by a wrinkled mass of skin sweating pink stuff.

The little voice in the back of my head was about to

give me hell for not being more observant, and for not thinking at all. Arlene saved it the trouble with a scream. I didn't blame her for screaming. I screamed too, the moment my brain started firing on all cylinders. The nitwit who came up with the idea that a strong woman should never scream had his head so far up his ass that daylight was a myth to him.

S&R didn't understand what had happened. They asked what had happened to the other units. They meant Hidalgo-Fly, and Hidalgo-Arlene. We tried to explain that the dying thing on the floor was Hidalgo. S&R would always have problems with the idea of death.

Arlene and I were more acquainted with that idea. Even as the blob of protoplasm begged for us to "finish" it, we were simultaneously firing our zap guns. The two beams of heat crossed each other, carving the blob into smaller pieces that didn't talk. We kept at it past the point of necessity.

"Why did you send new unit away?" asked S&R. The Klave mind found what had happened intriguing. They may have thought Hidalgo had been transformed into something closer to them, a duality of some kind. I didn't know. I didn't care.

The officer, the man Arlene had once considered spacing out an airlock, had proved himself one of Earth's best. He'd been the leader of our fire team. We owed him what we had just done for him.

Funny thing. He'd fought his quota of monsters. A steam demon had taken his wife. He'd kicked butt with hell-princes and spiders. On Phobos he was a bud, helping take down the imps and the flying skulls and the superpumpkin. He was a veteran of the Doom War.

And a freakin' teleporter nails him. Shit. A bleeding technological foul-up. It made me so mad I saw Mars-red. We owed him more than putting him out of his misery. We owed him words, a proper farewell due an honorable man.

We gave him a different kind of farewell, worthy of a good marine. Our first Freds made the bad mistake of showing up just then. I didn't leave any for Arlene or S&R. The ray guns made my job too easy.

Yeah, right. Isn't technology grand? It fries Hidalgo and then gives me a push-button method of avenging him. We kicked ass. Nothing made me feel better. The guns were light, and they didn't need reloading. S&R mentioned they'd need recharging eventually, but they were good for a thousand kills per charge. I tried my best to use it up.

A few Freds fired off a few saucers. Their aim was not up to Marine Corps standards.

S&R aimed at the Freds' chests to get the brain right away. When I realized the aliens could feel pain I started aiming for the artichoke heads and the arms and the legs. Arlene reminded me that we had a mission to perform. That didn't help. I'd been inactive too long, bottled up too much. Now it was payback time.

We came across two Freds making love. I recognized the process from S&R's lesson. Their normal height was six feet. When one extended to over seven feet, it was ready to copulate; but only if another one was ready to be on the receiving end. The tall one would find a mate that had shortened down to under five feet. Then the tall one would insert its pyramidal head into the cavity in shorty's head.

They shared genetic information that way. The

"male" turned bright red and the "female" turned a rich purple. A scientist would have found the demonstration endlessly fascinating. I found it more rewarding to interrupt the festivities by choosing my shots with imagination. Before they died, I'm certain these Freds felt some of what Hidalgo suffered.

While I was amusing myself, S&R and Arlene found the main computer and loaded the program. Then they found me in a room running with alien blood. The color reminded me of iced tea.

"What now?" I choked out the words. They tried to tell me the mission had been accomplished. This didn't cut it. We hadn't finished using our zap guns.

"We have no ship any longer," sighed Arlene. She turned to S&R and asked if they had any suggestions.

Those boys sure did. There were functional teleport pads on the base. In the immortal words of S&R, "Gateways must go to Fred ships. Not safe to go."

The little voice in my head pointed out that we had run out of enemies to kill here. At no point did it bother me to think that I was failing to snuff out mind-consciousnesses or ghost-spirits. These alien monsters were dead enough for me.

I shouldered the burden of command. Sergeant Taggart had a plan. "Let's go!" covered both my strategy and my tactics.

We booked. In my rage I forgot the ship would be in zero-g. But the moment I felt that old free fall spinning in my stomach, I reminded myself that the wonderful ray guns had no kick and were perfect weapons for this environment.

Too bad they didn't make the trip with us. Neither did our clothes or equipment. Yep, it was as if we'd gone through the Phobos Gate again. Stripped nekkid. There was Arlene to port, her long, firmly muscled legs kicking slightly as if she were swimming. Kid sure had a nice ass. And there were Sears and Roebuck. Naked, they looked even more like Magilla Gorilla. But their feet were far more human than simian. I'd wondered about that.

"What do we do now, Sergeant?" asked Arlene. She didn't say it like my best buddy. She said it like someone who has been thinking more clearly than her superior officer.

S&R came to my rescue. "We had no choice but to be remaining baseless."

While I tried to decide if that counted as a pun, Arlene began to cry. That was so unlike her that it helped bring me back to a semblance of sanity. I noticed her hand on her neck. Then I realized what was wrong. Her last link with Albert had been wiped out—the second ring, the honeymoon ring. No way could S&R re-create it outside their own lab.

We didn't have long to worry about that problem, however. The Freds on the ship soon noticed their stowaways-pirates-boarders. They had better aim than the ones at the base. They came clomping along the bulkhead in their magnetized boots, some below us, some above us. The saucers they were firing were coming closer and closer while we floated around, naked and helpless.

This was when I realized I could have done a better job of planning for contingencies. In the few seconds of life remaining, I gave some cursory attention to the ship. Details might come in useful in the next life, always assuming this death theory for humans was inadequate to cover the facts.

The ship was the same design as the Klave cruiser, but much longer. I'd guess it was 3.7 kilometers from stem to stern. The Fred spaceship had to be the largest cigar in the universe.

While we ducked little flying saucers, I quickly reviewed what I'd learned and deduced from S&R's briefing. They were too busy ducking to engage in dialogue, so I had to trust my memory.

S&R had never come right out and said it, but the Freds were more like humans than the Klave in one important respect—they too were individualists. This was carried to a lunatic extreme in the lack of cooperation among the demonic invaders. I'd lost count of how many times Arlene and I had saved ourselves by tricking the monsters into fighting each other. In a choice between slaughtering humans and trashing each other, hell-princes and pumpkins opted for the latter every time.

So if it had worked a hundred times before, why not try for one hundred and one? "Hand-to-hand combat!" I shouted. "I don't think they're that much stronger than we are." I was certain that none of us in this ship were as strong as S&R.

"Maybe we can grab one of their guns," suggested Arlene.

"No Fred guns can be used for going to kill by you," said S&R. It took a moment for their meaning to sink in—namely, that the weapons could be activated only by a Fred.

I set the example. Much as I hated zero-g, I'd spent so much time in it lately that I'd developed a knack for turning it to my advantage. A new form of martial arts could be developed in free fall.

Kicking off from the wall, I grabbed the nearest Fred and yanked that sucker right out of his magnetic boots. Momentum was on my side; it was my new pal.

I threw the alien into two of its comrades. They didn't act like pals. If they had any brains in those big chests, they'd have reasoned out what I was doing, then extrapolated from it and cooperated with one another.

What an irony. Arlene and I were two of the most rabid individualists any collectivist could ever have the misfortune to meet. The Klave collective had thrown in with their antithesis, Homo sapiens, against a common foe.

Could the ultimate error of the bad guys be their deconstructionism? They took everything apart, leaving no basis for rational self-interest.

Food for thought. Philosophy to while away the time after we cleansed this ship of its owners. S&R were using a different fighting technique. They were mainly crushing their opponents, and ripping out whole portions of the chest area. Arlene and I were succeeding in making the Freds fight among themselves.

Suddenly S&R called out a warning. The Fred coming up beneath me apparently wore an insignia S&R recognized as some kind of biological scientist, a med-Fred. When this one grabbed me and pulled me down, I could see that it understood something about our species.

Instead of jabbing its chopstick fingers toward my chest, where it might puncture my heart, it went for my brain, assuming the only real weakness of the Freds must also be a human weakness.

Never assume.

It jabbed one of its killer fingers into the area where it had learned humans keep their brains—the head. But this alien's research was slightly inadequate. The needle of pain hurt like blazes, as it went through my cheek, but he missed my brain by the side of a barn door.

Then it was my turn. I ripped into his head like it was a piece of rotten cabbage. I think it screamed as I kept working down, down, down to the part of a living thing that can anticipate bad things before they happen. I laughed. I was getting back to doing what I do best.

By some miracle we cleaned out the section we were in. Then we moved to the next. Although similar to the Klave ship in terms of engineering, the inside of this vessel was composed of separate compartments. As we floated from one section to the next, like angels of death, my theory received endless vindication: the Freds were not communicating with each other!

We simply repeated the process until our arms and legs were so tired we had to stop. Then we resumed our attack, and still the pods had not communicated with each other. Only at the end did we encounter a different sort of Fred.

This one might have been the captain of the ship. He was the smartest, and he had a weapon that almost wiped us out. "Look out for the Fred ray!" S&R shouted in one of their clearest sentences, saving Arlene and me from the brink of destruction. We pushed each other out of harm's way. While we bounced off the bulkheads and bobbed around like corks in a bottle, a searing beam of white energy missed us and melted one wall of the pod. Fortunately the integrity of the ship's bulkhead was not compromised.

S&R took care of this Fred personally. Four strong hands took the cabbage apart. Afterward we discovered we should have taken this one down first. But how were we to know this particular artichoke had access to the ship's main computer? Damned thing didn't even look like a computer. Looked like a blender to me.

The top Fred had programmed the ship to go . . . somewhere. There was nothing we could do to alter the program. We'd succeeded in killing all the Freds. But we were stuck on their Galaxy Express with a one-way ticket. Arlene was not happy about this.

Epilogue

I will never see Albert again. I'd reconciled myself to accepting him as a sixty-seven-year-old. I could have still loved him. At least we would have been together again.

But Fly had to take the mission to the limit. I saw that berserker look come over him after Hidalgo died, and I understood. I also knew we might not have come through alive without that fire in him. When I can think again, I'll tell Fly I understand.

Now I can only feel my loss. By the time we arrive at our destination and turn around, Albert will have been in his grave for centuries. So I sit alone at one end of the ship while Fly sits at the other. The Fred ship has large picture windows.

I watch the stars contract to a small red disk at the center of the line of travel. Fly watches a similar disk, but his is blue. We do not talk. He searches for words that I do not want to hear.

We both wonder what the human race will do in the next several thousand years.